Battle Ready

Equipping and Encouraging the Teens in God's Army

by J.E. Solinski

Take the HELMET of SALVATION

Battle Ready
by J.E. Solinski

Copyright © 2025 Jody Eileen Solinski.

This book is a work of fiction. Names, characters, places, and incidents are the product of the author's imagination and are used factiously. Any resemblance to actual events, locales, or persons, living or dead, is coincidental.

J.E. Solinski books may be purchased through
www.jesolinski.com or Amazon.com.
Book design by Pamela Lee.

All rights reserved. No part of this book may be used or reproduced by any means, graphics, electronic, or mechanical, including photocopying, recording, taping or by any information storage retrieval system without the written permission of the publisher except in the case of brief quotations embodied in critical articles and reviews. For information, email info@jesolinski.com.

Unless otherwise noted, all scripture is from THE HOLY BIBLE, NEW INTERNATIONAL VERSION®, NIV® Copyright © 1973, 1978, 1984, 2011 by Biblica, Inc.® Used by permission. All rights reserved worldwide. Some Scripture taken from the New King James Version® Copyright © 1982 by Thomas Nelson. Used by permission. All rights reserved.

Scripture quotations marked as NKJV have been taken from The Holy Bible: New King James Version® Copyright © 1982 by Thomas Nelson. Used by permission. All rights reserved.

ISBN: 979-8-9926225-1-5
Library of Congress Control Number: 2018952390

First Edition
September 2025

AMOC PUBLICATIONS™

*To all my students over the years.
I have drawn from your experiences and your hearts.*

Note to Reader

The stories in this collection span twenty-five years of writing. Therefore, many of the stories won't have cell phones or computers or other current technology. While some struggles are unique to a certain generation because of the technology or the lack of it, most of the challenges the teens in these stories face are common to all generations. I hope you enjoy them and take away a kernel of truth from each one.

Therefore put on the full armor of God, so that when the day of evil comes, you may be able to stand your ground, and after you have done everything, to stand.

[14] Stand firm then, with the belt of truth buckled around your waist, with the breastplate of righteousness in place, [15] and with your feet fitted with the readiness that comes from the gospel of peace. [16] In addition to all this, take up the shield of faith, with which you can extinguish all the flaming arrows of the evil one.

[17] **Take the helmet of salvation** and the sword of the Spirit, which is the word of God.

(Ephesians 6:13–17)

Table of Contents

As We Forgive Our Debtors 9
A Delicate Balance 17
A Good Friend Would... 23
All That Money Can Buy 31
Camp Contentment.. 37
Follow the Rules... 45
Friends.. 51
Gifts.. 57
I am Bryan's Brain 65
Line Call... 71
More than Muscle 79
New Girl... 85
Pressure 93
Read the Manual... 99
Something Stinks.. 105
Soul Support... 113
Spiritual Muscles.. 119
The Race... 127
The War of the Carrots 135
Then Sings My Soul 141

As We Forgive Our Debtors

"Our Father in heaven, Hallowed be Your name. Your kingdom come, Your will be done On earth as it is in heaven. Give us this day our daily bread. And forgive us our debts, as we forgive our debtors. And do not lead us into temptation, But deliver us from the evil one. For Yours is the kingdom and the power and the glory forever. Amen." (NKJV)

Without too much thought, Jimmy recited the Lord's Prayer along with the rest of the congregation. He had learned it in the second grade, and like the flag salute, it was second nature to him. That gave him the chance to keep one eye open and check out the sanctuary. He was careful to look only ahead of him. If his mother heard his voice coming from a variety of directions, she would get suspicious.

He ran his eye along the rows in front of him until he spotted the dark brown hair he had been hunting for. Allison was only four rows ahead. He let out a sigh of relief and closed his eyes while the pastor finished up with a prayer of his own.

He and Allison had been dating for over a year, and the relationship was feeling pretty comfortable. He knew that mushroom and olive was her favorite pizza topping and that ice cream her favorite food. He knew never to take her to a movie starring Ben Affleck but not to miss one with Ryan Gosling. He knew that she loved softball and that she studied like a warhorse. He also knew that he could basically count on a date every Saturday night unless her family was out of town and that her family usually sat about four rows ahead of his *and* that her parents were adamant about the family sitting together during service. Yup, he knew her pretty well.

He listened halfheartedly to the sermon. After all, it was spring, and there were so many other, more important issues to be thinking about. Baseball season had just started, trout season was just around the corner, and Allison's birthday was next weekend. No, too much on the mind to zero in on the lesson. The final hymn was sung, and he stood up and stretched his aching legs.

One more prayer and we're out of here, he thought happily.

With the final "amen," he headed out of the pew ahead of his parents and into the fresh spring air. He threw his head back and took a deep, refreshing drink of it.

"Careful, someone could come up and punch you right in the gut," a voice said and then playfully did it just to prove his point.

"Oooofff," Jimmy said, straightening up and looking straight into the eyes of his best friend, Rob Larsen. Rob was grinning from ear to ear.

"I could have hit you a lot harder," Rob said.

"But you wouldn't dare," Jimmy replied, knowing he had a fifteen-pound edge and four-inch reach on Rob, but he protected his stomach just the same.

"You're right," Rob said, "but let's get down to business." And the grin reappeared. "How would you," he said pointing at Jimmy, "like to join me, my dad, and my uncle next weekend up on the Klamath River for the first day of trout season."

Jimmy's eyes lit up. "Wow! That would be great!" he answered and then his face dropped suddenly. "But I can't."

Rob looked at him incredulously. "What do you mean, you can't?"

Jimmy shrugged. "I promised to take Allison out."

"But you take her out every weekend. Surely she'd give you your freedom back for this."

Jimmy glared at his best friend. He didn't like the insinuation packed into that last sentence.

"I still have my freedom," he countered. "It's just that it's her birthday Saturday, and I've already made reservations at the Hatch Cover and all, and …"

"Well, cancel them," Rob said. "She'd understand."

"Not on her birthday."

"Then make something up," he suggested. "Say your grandfather's ill, and you have to go out of town. Come on. You're a bright boy. Think of something."

Jimmy fell silent. He could probably think of an excuse that Allison might buy, but—

"I don't know," he said. "I did that once before, remember? When I broke our date so that a bunch of us could go bowling? She found out."

"Yeah, but she forgave you. You're still together, aren't you? So what's the big deal?"

"She was pretty mad," he answered. *Not because I broke the date,* he reflected, *but because I had lied to her.* Not a great trust-building move.

"Okay, it's your life," Rob answered. "But let me know by Wednesday if you haven't been released from bondage, so I can invite someone else."

He turned and walked away, and Jimmy watched him go, feeling both the sting of his words and the lure of the trip. He probably could think of something that wouldn't make Allison suspicious and be partially true. He released a deep sigh.

"Opening day of trout season only happens once a year," a little voice on his left shoulder whispered.

"But then so does Allison's birthday," said a little voice on his right shoulder.

He had only a few minutes to stew over his dilemma

before Allison joined him in front of the church.

"You look like you're enjoying the sun," she said.

"Yeah," he replied, short on words while trying to fabricate a valid excuse to break their date.

"Do you have a minute?" she asked. "I need to talk to you."

"Sure," he said. "Shoot."

"It's about this weekend," she said, and Jimmy felt his heart sink. It was only going to get worse, he thought.

"Yeah?" he asked cautiously.

"I don't think I can make our date," she said. "Since it's my eighteenth birthday, mom's having a big family get together."

Jimmy felt the ton of bricks start to fall from his shoulders, but then waited. Was he now expected to come to the family gathering? He felt sweat form around his neck. They weren't *that* serious he didn't think.

Allison smiled wanly. "I'd invite you over, but I think it might be a bit overwhelming, and well, I wouldn't be able to devote much time to you. We have a big family."

The bricks fell, and Jimmy tried hard to look a little disappointed.

"Hey, no problem," he said. "I totally understand. We'll celebrate the following weekend."

"Are you sure?" she asked tentatively. "I know you made plans and all."

Jimmy shook his head. "Easy to change."

She gave him a quick kiss on the cheek. "You're the greatest," she said. "I'll call you later."

"Sure thing," he said as she bounced away.

Within an hour he had confirmed the trout trip with Rob.

・ ・ ・

The weekend couldn't have been better. They left Friday night and camped so close to the river they could have cast their lines from their sleeping bags. When the sun peeked over the ridge, they already had their lines in the water.

By the time Saturday night came and they headed home, each fisherman had caught his limit, and Jimmy felt on top of the world.

・ ・ ・

"You and Allison still going out?" Brian McKay asked over the back of the pew.

Jimmy turned to look at Brian carefully.

"Yeah. Why?"

Brian's fair skin deepened into an embarrassed red.

"Oh, no reason really," he stammered and slid back into his seat.

Jimmy turned further to face him and stared hard at the younger boy.

"Why?" he repeated more forcefully, and the boy folded.

"It's just that I saw her at the movies Saturday night

with this other guy, a big blond, and another couple, and I just assumed ...." Brian's voice faded off into a miserable silence.

Now it was Jimmy's face that began to burn a bright red. The organ music began to play. Brian slid further into his seat, and Jimmy turned to face the pulpit.

She cheated on me, Jimmy fumed. *She lied and then cheated on me. Family get-together, my eye. She just made up that story so she could go out with this other clown. Man, I must look the fool. Probably the laughing stock of the whole town. Well, we'll see who comes out the winner on this. Allison's history.*

His mind was churning with all the things he would say to her and the looks he would throw her way. He tried to see the back of that dark brown hair four pews ahead, but her family wasn't in their normal spot. He quickly looked around but couldn't see them anywhere.

Probably didn't come," he thought. *Probably feeling miserably guilty.* Hopefully as miserable as he was feeling.

"Please bow with me," came the pastor's directive, and Jimmy's head went down, but his mind didn't take in even one of the pastor's prayer requests, yet when he heard the familiar lines, "to pray in the manner He taught us to pray," Jimmy, as though on autopilot, joined in with the rest of the congregation.

The words spilled off his tongue but were nowhere near his mind, until—

"… and forgive us our debts, as we also have forgiven our debtors."

The last word caught in the back of his throat. What had he just said? Forgive us the way we forgive others? Despite the combined warmth of the sanctuary and his own anger, Jimmy shuddered. Did God really work that way? If He did, then Jimmy was in big trouble. He thought about what to do.

Though he was hurt by Allison's betrayal, and it might be the end of their relationship, deep in his heart, right where the pain had settled, he knew he would have to forgive her.

When the service finally ended, Jimmy made his way out to the parking lot, hoping the fresh spring air would revive his spirits. He was almost beginning to feel better when he saw Allison walking toward him and next to her was this huge Nordic god.

So she is *here,* he thought, and not only here, but here with him! He felt anger rise just as his heart sank once again. *What gall. Bringing the new guy right to him. Is this her way of coming clean? Of being honest?* If it was, he knew he wasn't keen on it.

"Jimmy," she said cheerfully, and then turned toward the handsome guy next to her. "I'd like you to meet my cousin, Michael, from Minnesota."

A Delicate Balance

Janet stopped on the narrow, rocky trail, and gazed peacefully at the scene around her. Where she stood now was merely a mountainside of shale. The noon sun was warm despite a strong breeze coming down off the mountain, and she looked back over the trail she had just traversed.

About a mile away, precariously perched atop one of the ridges, stood the lookout she had just left. Ahead of her rose mighty Mr. Rainier, its snow- and glacier-covered peak almost touchable. This was her favorite spot on the trip so far. She started walking again, a smile playing on her lips. A month ago, she wouldn't have dreamed of saying that. A month ago she was fighting to stay home.

• • •

"But why do *I* have to go?" Janet almost screamed. "Now my entire summer is ruined. I'll have to give up my job. I'm sixteen. I can stay by myself!"

"But you won't," her father replied firmly. "This is a

family vacation, and the whole family is going. You knew that before you ever took the job."

Yeah, but I thought if I had one, you'd change your mind and let me stay, she thought sullenly.

The camping trip around the Western U.S. and Canada had been planned for three years now. The family had foregone taking any extended vacations so that both parents could save up a six-week block of time. Three years ago, when she was thirteen, it had sounded great, but now it sounded like a bore. Six weeks, thirty-five days, eight hundred and forty hours, fifty thousand and four hundred minutes, to be exact, of camping, driving, and just being around parents. Add to the mix two brothers, aged twelve and eight, and you had more than any teenager should have to endure.

It was more for the boys anyway, she rationalized. They liked camping and fishing and hiking. Of course, she had too, three years ago, but that was before high school. Now she liked boys, and if she wanted boys to like her, she knew she needed to focus on looking good, not traipsing off on adventures.

Which brought up the big problem of the summer. Gary Cook. He was the reason she had applied to Taco Time and the real reason she wanted to stay home and work. But all that was ruined now because of a stupid family vacation. In fact, now her whole life was ruined.

Despite her moping around, she still found herself in the

car at four o'clock Monday morning as the family left, hoping to cross most of the desert before the heat set in.

The first week Janet played the role of the martyr perfectly and refused to take in any of the activities Hoover Dam, the Grand Canyon, or Zion National Park had to offer. Her parents let her sit at the campsite and pout while they hiked and looked around.

By the time they reached Bryce National Park, the second week, Janet was begrudgingly taking part in the family excursions, though she refused to look like she was enjoying herself. But the splashing display of colors at Bryce, the open ruggedness of the Grand Tetons, and the wonders of Yellowstone melted her stubborn reserve, and as they drove past the rolling farmlands of Montana on their way to Glacier National Park, her love of the outdoors was just too strong, and she dropped the facade all together and began enjoying herself.

She fished in Waterton Lake, whooped it up at the Stampede in Calgary, hiked forever in the Canadian Rockies around Banff and Jasper, and gazed in awe at the beauty of Butchart Gardens on Vancouver Island. But Mt. Rainier, with its alpine setting, was definitely her favorite. They camped next to the White River, perfectly named for its almost opaque white water, straight from the melting glacier.

Daily, she and her family hiked, enjoying the native wildflowers—lupine, Indian paintbrush, monkey flower—

that grew in the shadow of the massive mountain. And each night around the campfire, her father would lead the family through a small devotional asking each member to relate what wonder of God he or she had seen that day.

The first week, Janet had had little to contribute, since she had spent most of her days in self-exile at the campsite, but as the trip progressed, she became more and more aware of God's infinite wisdom in creating His world, a world delicately balanced, placing the most fragile of his creations next to the most massive.

Here at Rainier, she had spent hours in the Visitor Center, pouring over the exhibits, memorizing every flower, every trail, every native creature. She hiked most of the trails, and her family, tired of three days of walking, had agreed to break camp while she took the five-mile round trip hike to the lookout.

It had been worth it, and now as she crested the ridge and began her final descent, she could see the family car in the parking lot ready to go. She quickened her pace. They wanted to be at Mt. St. Helens by early afternoon.

The drive to Mt. St. Helens was a disappointment. Janet had expected to see signs of devastation and destruction all along the way, but everything looked surprisingly healthy and ordinary. Even after they had taken the turnoff and were only about ten miles from the crater itself the world looked untouched.

Finally, a sign for a scenic view emerged, and Mr.

Stanton pulled off the road into the parking lot. Still nothing. It was not until they had walked right to the rim of the overlook, that they saw the result of the blast that was 2,500 times greater than the bomb that destroyed Hiroshima.

A vast wasteland of ash and debris lay before them. Trees that used to be hundreds of feet tall and two to three feet thick lay like broken matchsticks across the endless miles, effortlessly snapped in half.

Janet slowly took in the scene. Where she stood nothing had been harmed. Yet only two feet away, as though an imaginary line had been drawn across the mountains, everything was destroyed. One tree lay lifeless on the ground. Another right next to it stood tall, complete, whole, untouched.

The family returned to the car and drove through the miles of devastation, past memorials for individuals caught not by the heat or debris, but by the poisonous gases that had travelled the eight miles in less than a minute.

Janet continued to stare. For weeks she had seen God's intricate workmanship in nature's delicately balanced ecosystem. Now she was witnessing just a touch of His awesome power that not even man had as yet been able to duplicate.

They passed Spirit Lake, now covered with broken logs and ash. Yet even as they drove, silently surveying the destruction around them, Janet could see new signs of life. Ten years after the eruption, the area still looked dead, but life had taken a stand and was tenaciously struggling to come back, attesting to God's power to bring life and hope to even the most lifeless and hopeless of situations. Fireweed and lupine were sprouting around broken tree trunks.

In the midst of this awesome display of power, Janet felt God's presence—His omniscience and omnipotence. Suddenly all her problems and worries seemed petty and insignificant.

A God who could create from nothing, destroy with a word, and then breathe life back into that devastation was surely a God who could love limitlessly, see everything, and solve anything. A God who could do all that could handle anything in her life, even something as life-shaking as six weeks away from a boyfriend. That was a God worthy of her adoration and trust.

A Good Friend Would

I poured myself a big glass of soda and plopped down on the sofa. Church was over, dinner finished, and the afternoon football games about to start. My Bengals were set to take on their Central Division rivals the Cleveland Browns in an all important, early-season meeting.

Cleveland signaled they were ready. The referee blew the whistle and the Browns' kicker stepped in and booted the ball. It was a high but short kick. Carl Pickens stepped in, took it on the 15-yard line, and headed to the right. Thomas threw a great block, which freed Pickens for another fifteen yards until he was finally brought down on his own 30-yard line.

"Yahoo!" I yelled. "Let's get 'em boys."

Dad heard my cheer. "Has the game started already?" he called from the kitchen.

"Just now," I shouted back. "Bengals' ball on their own thirty."

"I'll be right there."

Sunday afternoon football was a tradition with my dad

and me. Being the only two males in a houseful of women (five to be exact), we have had to stick together. Mom calls this our time of male bonding. Of course, the girls like football too and would be right next to us if we let them, but we don't. They can watch the college games on Saturday with us. But on Sunday, it's just Dad and me.

They're fine with it and will watch with their friends or on the TV in my parents' room if they really want to see the game.

"Bengals! Bengals!" I yelled in my deepest voice just as a hand-off was made to the running back who scooted around the left side for another 12-yard pickup. "Yeah!" I yelled and jumped to my feet, did a little end zone dance, and, to put it simply, acted like a complete idiot. But then, this was football.

"Anything happen so far?" Dad asked as he joined me with his own soda and a large bowl of popcorn. It mattered little that we had left the dinner table only ten minutes earlier. Popcorn and soda were a must.

"Only that we've moved 27 yards in less than ten seconds," I said smugly. "The Browns will eat dirt today. Phil Cox in particular," I added with a wry grin.

I held my breath as the Bengals' quarterback dropped back to pass. "McGee! He's clear!" I yelled. "Pass it to him! Pass it to him!" Quarterback Jeff Blake must have heard me because he let fly a perfect spiral right across the middle to where tight end Tony McGee was cutting across the flat under the zone. McGee caught the ball in full stride and then cut up field, broke one tackle, spun around and evaded another, and then raced twenty more yards before finally being caught by the free safety.

"Bengals! Bengals!" I yelled jumping to my feet. The phone rang.

"Since you're up, would you mind getting that?" my father stated calmly. He hadn't moved since he had sat down. A real Mr. Excitement.

I grumbled under my breath as I moved to get the phone, keeping one eye glued to the TV.

"Hello?" I said, and then, "YES!" as a Bengal eluded a would-be tackler and ran for five.

"Matt?"

My heart dropped to my fallen arches. It was Robert.

"Yeah," I answered about as unenthusiastically as I could.

"Are you busy?"

Every fiber in my body wanted to say "yes," but I couldn't.

"Not really," I answered. "What's up?"

The other end of the line hesitated. "Are you sure?"

Now I was getting peeved.

"I said I wasn't. What's up?"

Another hesitation. I knew my tone of voice and my words were throwing contradictory messages across the line, but I was missing my football game.

"NO!" my father yelled, and I turned in time to see a Browns' defender run the opposite direction with the ball. An interception! Things were sliding downhill fast.

"What's up, Robert?" I asked again. My voice edged with irritation.

"It's my dad," he said. "Do you think we could get together and do something?"

My heart sank. Now what? A good friend would invite him over, but this was a dad-me thing, and I tended to get a little selfish about stuff like that. Still …

"You want to come over here?" I asked, gritting my teeth. "My dad and I are just watching the game."

Silence. "I'd rather not. Can we just shoot a few baskets at the school?"

Now my whole body went limp. There went my Sunday completely; the one day of the week I looked forward to. "Sure," I said, trying to muster some enthusiasm. "I'll meet you there in ten."

"Thanks, buddy," he said, and I could hear the gratefulness in his voice.

"No problem," I lied, and I knew he could tell.

Now I guess I should explain. I met Robert a year ago when he moved to Cincinnati, and we became pretty good friends. Anything I suggested, he agreed to, as long as it got him out of his house. That was before I knew his family history and how it was going to disrupt my life.

His father is an alcoholic and gets pretty abusive when

he's drunk. It wouldn't have been too bad if all we did was have fun and goof around. But with Robert came all the problems with his father, which he needed to talk about, and I wasn't really up to it half of the time. I know a good friend would, and probably should, but I felt a little put upon, so more than once I had made up some lame excuse or another to get out of spending time with him.

As I walked to the school, slamming the basketball into every pile of dead leaves I came to, I also knew why he didn't want to come over to my house. Being with my dad was just another reminder of what he *didn't* have.

By the time I reached the school, though, my disappointment had subsided somewhat. The cool September air cleared my brain. But not until I saw Robert sitting dejectedly on the bench did I feel guilty for my selfishness. When he heard the ball hit the asphalt, his head popped up and a look of appreciation flooded his face. At that moment I really felt for the guy. He stood up, and I tossed the ball to him, then peeled off my sweatshirt.

"How 'bout a nice short game of *Mississippi* to warm up," I said grinning.

Robert smiled a genuine smile of relief.

"Thanks for coming, Matt," he said. "I really appreciate it. I know it's Sunday and your dad and all that, and then the Bengals are play—"

I waved him off. "It's nothing," I said, and for the first time that afternoon I was being honest with him. "They can win without me yelling at the TV, and I *know* they can lose without me."

He laughed and when he stopped, we both just looked at each other for a minute. Hopelessness hung heavy in the air. As much as I tried to fight it, I could feel the Holy Spirit working on me.

Tell him. Tell him. I squirmed, and I knew why too. Though I had known Robert for over a year, I had never invited him to church and never shared Christ with him. I was scared to. Not scared of what he might think, but scared of what extra responsibilities I might inherit. I mean, I was already buried under a load of his misery. If he decided to accept Christ, I might have to help disciple him, share with him Christ's perspective. In other words, I might have to live out my Christian rhetoric and become more involved. According to my timetable, I really didn't have the time or energy for all that.

A good friend would, the Holy Spirit nudged.

I squirmed again.

The Holy Spirit was right. Friends share stuff, especially good stuff. When I found this new graphing calculator that made trig easier, I told Robert about it. When hunting season opened, we took him to the best zone we knew. I even talked him out of signing up for Mr. Mackey's history class. The guy really owed me for that one. So really, why wouldn't I share the most important thing in my life with him?

"How about Pony?" he said weakly, not at all sure it would alleviate his pain.

I shook my head, and he looked at me confused. Hadn't I suggested *Mississippi*?

"Around the World?" he ventured.

I shook my head again, and now Robert looked pained.

"Not just yet," I said by way of explanation. "I've been playing too many games with you, Robert," I confessed. "I think it's time I leveled with you." I gestured toward at the benches. "I've been holding out on you, buddy."

He looked at me confused, as we moved to the benches.

"I've got a really good Friend that I would like to introduce you to," I said, paused, and then added, "at least a good friend would."

All That Money Can Buy

"Hey, Gary! You want to come over and see my new stereo system?"

"New?" I asked. To my recollection, he had just bought a new system less than a year ago.

"Yeah, I just bought it. You've got to see it. It is so sweet sounding."

"But didn't you—"

"Obsolete," Matt interjected cutting me off, slightly irritated. He knew what I was going to say. He had heard it before. "Come over, and I'll show you what I mean." The excitement was back in his voice.

"Sure, I'll be right over."

"And bring a couple of your tapes or CDs," he added, "so you can witness the difference."

I agreed, hung up, and grabbed a couple of tapes. Matt knew I didn't own any CDs. It took me about half an hour to get to his place. He lives across town in the Country Club Estates, in one of those huge, four thousand square foot Tudor-style homes with a black bottom pool and five cars parked out front.

I, on the other hand, don't live in anything that remotely resembles an estate or a club. I couldn't even qualify for the country, but I didn't care. Mom, besides working part time, always keeps the house clean and cooks us good meals. Dad works hard and provides us with everything we need. We are a little shy sometimes on what we might want, but we are happy. I have often wondered why Matt picked me out to be his friend. We have very little in common.

He's rich; I'm not. He's into swimming and water polo—I play basketball. He's on his fourth stereo system in as many years, and I'm still saving up to buy my first one. He isn't a Christian, and I am. When I think back, I can't even remember how we became friends. It was like all of a sudden he was around, and that was that.

The bus let me off about a mile away from his subdivision, and I walked the rest of the way. Even though it was cold out, I enjoyed the walk. I admired the huge homes, the sleek sports cars, and the spacious, manicured lawns. These people seemed to lack nothing, but whenever they came rushing out of their doors, tennis racket or briefcase in hand, I rarely saw a smile. Worry, frustration, anger. Those were the more common expressions.

I walked up the Norris driveway, stopping to look at Matt's vintage red 1964 Mustang. He always had to have the best … or the first.

The doorbell rang deep and long, one of those chimed numbers like grandfather clocks have. I was surprised to see Mrs. Norris answer the door. Usually, it was Carmen their housekeeper. Mrs Norris looked a little harried.

"Why hello, Gary," she said pleasantly enough. "Matt's in his room. Why don't you go on back."

"Thank you," I answered. "Where's Carmen?"

The question brought a weariness back into her eyes and a droop of her shoulders. "Sick, I'm afraid, and I'm having a terrible time keeping up with it all. I just hate housework."

I gave her a sympathetic smile and thought of my own mother. I'm sure she didn't like cleaning toilets much, but at least she did it with a smile.

"Do your work as unto the Lord," she had said one day when I asked her if she enjoyed housework. And then with a wink of an eye added, "Heaven knows you men don't care."

Actually, we did, but I guess we just never said anything. I made it a point after that to mention it to her every once in a while.

I walked into Matt's room, and he was enmeshed in a spaghetti mess of wire.

"Hi, Matt," I said. He turned with some difficulty but smiled just the same. There was that excited gleam in his eye that he got whenever he had a new toy. I knew the routine. I had seen it before, with the Mustang, the Minolta camera, the ten-speed.

"Here, grab this wire and hold it for me," he instructed, and I stepped in obediently while he went back to work. "I'll have this set up in a jiffy," he said, "and then wait till you hear it."

It did take him only a matter of minutes, and then we placed the wires behind the cabinets and pushed the wall unit into place. I had to admit, the new system with its sleek black casing and LED display looked sharp. The "old" system lay discarded on the bed.

"Give me one of your tapes," he said, and I handed him Michael W. Smith's. It was one of the few Christian artists he would listen to. He stuck it in the cassette player and turned it on. The music began to filter out of the speakers, and Matt began fooling with this dial and that: equalizers, enhancers, Dolby. Finally, he stepped back.

"Now does that sound sweet or what?" he asked.

I listened intently. It did sound good. The music came to us from all corners of the room.

"Now don't tell me you can't tell the difference between this sound and what that piece of junk produced," he said nodding toward the bed.

I glanced at the offending stereo system lying pathetically on the bed. Actually that piece of junk was a whole lot better than what I intended to buy, and if the truth be told, my ear couldn't discriminate *any* difference though I was sure there was one. I just smiled and decided to focus on Michael's music. Matt figured out I hadn't noticed a difference and jumped up to insert a different tape.

"You can really tell the difference with this one," he said and pressed the play button. I nodded like I did, but I didn't. He read my mind.

"It *really* makes a difference with CDs," he insisted, and pulled one from his stash of hundreds. This went on all afternoon as we listened to bits of one tape and snatches of a CD. Never once did we sit back and listen to a whole song through. Around four o'clock Matt tired of it.

"Let's go for a spin," he suggested. "I just had the seats reupholstered. It looks and rides great."

I chastened myself for not having noticed when I walked by, but then the old seats hadn't looked bad. I followed Matt out to the car, and the conversation turned from electronics to engines in a matter of seconds. The stereo was forgotten, and I realized I really didn't want to go for a spin. There were some things at home that I needed to get done.

"How 'bout a rain check on the ride," I said after I had checked out and admired the new leather. "I've got a bunch of homework I need to get started on."

Matt's face fell in disappointment, but he put on a pretty good facade.

"How about I drive you home?" he asked. I smiled but declined.

Already bought a round-trip bus fair," I said.

"Sure," he said shrugging it off. "Maybe tomorrow."

I shook my head.

"I have church in the morning, and then we kind of reserve Sunday for the family. How about next weekend?"

Matt nodded and then turned to head for the house. I walked down the driveway, but turned back to watch him. He stopped to shoot a couple of baskets, then went over to look in the boat before disappearing through the front door. Suddenly, it occurred to me why I was Matt's friend.

I had something he didn't, and he knew it. He wanted it and was trying every possible way to get it, only it couldn't be bought.

Though I didn't have hundreds of dollars to fill my room with new gadgets each week, my life was full of peace and contentment because of my relationship with Jesus. Matt's wasn't. His was a vacuum filled only momentarily with the thrill of a new purchase and then empty again once that newness wore off.

That was the beauty of a relationship with Christ. It never grew old, only better. It was never obsolete or outdated. That's what David meant in Psalm 19:10 when he said that God's laws were "more precious than gold."

I really think Matt knew what I had, but he hadn't yet come to the realization that he couldn't buy it. It was something that was already purchased for him. All he had to do was accept it.

Camp Contentment

"… four hundred and thirty-two, four hundred and thirty-three, four hundred and …."

Heidi walked down the worn, dusty trail following five ten-year-old girls, three of whom were locked arm-in-arm and counting each step.

Why is it kids this age count everything? she wondered, waving her hand in front of her, trying to disperse the dust they were kicking up. Though they were walking, none of them were lifting their feet.

They had counted every step on the way to the lake—5,627 in all—counted how many of them could fit into the outhouse there—12— and now insisted on counting the steps back, as though it was going to change drastically in three hours. No doubt they counted every highway deflector on the way up to camp too, driving their parents crazy. They were certainly driving *her* crazy.

She removed her straw hat and wiped her brow with her bare arm. Boy, it was hot. Though Camp Discovery was situated in a little valley in the Sierra Nevada, its elevation of 3,586 didn't protect it from the hot California sun. Without stopping, she pulled the canteen from her hip, opened it, and took a swig, keeping her eyes on the stragglers ahead of her. Aided by the glaring midday sun, the resentment that had been churning in her veins now boiled.

"Why do I always get stuck with the glory jobs?" she grumbled, looking up ahead where Marcia White, a.k.a. Spurs, was leading the group. Around her clustered a group of ten-year-olds, all vying for her attention and affection, and she wasn't disappointing any of them. Behind them came the three "counters," followed by the two stragglers, followed by Heidi eating everybody's dust.

"I'm tired," complained one whisper of a girl. "Do we have to walk *all* the way back?"

"How else do you expect to get back?" Heidi asked, trying hard to keep the irritation out of her voice. She had little tolerance for kids who signed up for a hike and then whined the entire time.

"We could stop at the road and have the others send the truck back for us," the girl suggested, dropping back with Heidi and then slowing her pace even more.

Heidi dropped her hand behind the young girl's back and gave her a gentle, but solid, push forward.

"I don't think so," Heidi answered. "Here. Have a drink. You'll feel better if you do."

The girl whined that she wouldn't. Heidi bit her lip trying not to respond. It would do no good to lose her temper.

"Guppy, how's it going back there?" Spurs had turned around in mid-stride and was now walking backward, looking over the line of girls behind her. "Everybody okay?" Her smile was broad and infectious but only wrought deeper resentment in Heidi.

"OK," she lied, smiling sweetly and waving, but the minute Spurs had turned around, the smile disappeared. *Why did I ever volunteer to do this?* she wondered.

At first being an assistant camp counselor for a week had sounded like a great idea. Her youth group was always looking for ways to serve and when the announcement came that Camp Discovery needed assistant counselors for their junior camps, Heidi was one of the first to sign up. She loved the outdoors and still had wonderful memories of her own camp experiences. With her swimming background, they had snatched her up, assigned her to the waterfront to help with lessons and life guarding, and bestowed her with the camp nickname "Guppy." In addition, she would assist Marcia in Joy cabin.

She had liked Marcia immediately. She was warm and friendly and for a nineteen-year-old extremely sure of herself. The evening and morning before the kids arrived, they set up their cabin and then Marcia gave Heidi a brief tour of the camp facilities. By the time the kids came

Sunday afternoon, Heidi was looking forward to a week of making a difference for kids, of being looked up to and admired both as a Christian and a person. But that dream died soon afterward.

The eight girls of Joy cabin had instinctively flocked to Marcia, trying not to cling, but to be as close as their ten-year-old mores would allow. Marcia had gathered them all to her, her warm, outgoing personality and mothering instincts providing just the needed insurance from homesickness. Heidi had felt desperately left out, even though Marcia had quickly introduced her as the other cabin counselor. The girls had smiled politely and then quickly returned their affections back to Marcia. She had pulled out her guitar and played for them, her rich soprano singing out some of the camp songs they would learn and encouraging them to join in. By dinnertime, Joy cabin was a solid, cohesive group. Well, almost.

• • •

Heidi coughed. As the hike forged on, the girls dragged their feet all the more, and the dust was getting pretty thick near the rear. She felt dirty and, undoubtedly, she looked worse. She would enjoy being back at the water this afternoon to wash half of the earth's crust off her.

Finally, the roofs of the cabins appeared below them, and the girls let out a cheer. Meryl, the complainer, groaned in relief and informed Heidi that she didn't think she was going to make it. Heidi gave her another persuasive push forward.

"Sure you will," she said tightly.

Lunch was uneventful. Not much excitement in bologna and cheese, and by this time even the camp punch had lost its novelty. Everyone headed back to their cabins for the required afternoon quiet hour. Monday this directive was met with groans and protests, but by today, Friday, most of the campers, and *all* of the counselors, looked forward to a brief spell out of the sun.

Heidi settled back on her bunk and watched Marcia make a quick round of the cabin, making sure everyone was set, tickling one here, giving a hug there, taking away the obnoxious corn nuts from the corner bunk. Each girl responded and Heidi winced inside. More than anything she wished she could be a head counselor and feed off of her young charges' affections. Though as a waterfront worker she had taught many to rid their fear of the water and others how to swim, she hadn't had the time to develop that close rapport Marcia had with the girls. She felt the resentment and bitterness that had boiled within her on the return hike resurface.

It just isn't fair! she thought, but she knew it wasn't right to feel this way, so she reached for her Bible. She had no idea where to look, so she opened to Matthew 1 and read the long, boring list of names again, recognizing some, but the majority she knew little about.

"Well, that helped a lot," she grumbled after completing the first chapter, and she set the Bible back down.

• • •

The searing hot of the morning became penetrating by afternoon, and the refreshing cool lake water washed away much of Heidi's frustration. She helped two eight-year-olds learn to breathe without stopping to raise their heads clear out of the water, taught one of the older girls to do a back dive off the pier, and set up a slalom course for the paddle boarders. But when it was time to take over the lifeguard's chair, the old depression returned. Her position high above the girls was a physical reminder of the emotional distance between them.

When the camp bell sounded the end of the afternoon activities, everyone headed up to their cabins to get ready for their last dinner of the week and the final campfire. Heidi, still burdened with her feelings of inadequacies and resentment walked to the chow hall behind little clusters of giddy girls. *What I wouldn't do to be one of the adored,* she thought despondently and took her seat with the rest of her cabin.

Dinner that night was a wonderful surprise. After a week of hamburger, spaghetti, and diluted camp punch, tonight was a wonderful feast of barbecue chicken, rice pilaf, corn on the cob, and real soda. Heidi, like everyone else in the hall, savored each mouthful.

When all had finished, one of the head counselors stood up and broke out singing the age-old camp song of appreciation, and everyone else joined in.

*Cookies, Cookies,
listen while we sing to you.
Cookies, Cookies,
you're a part of camp life too.
Anyone can make a bed,
and anyone can sweep,
but it takes our Cookies
to make us things to eat, so
Cookies, Cookies,
listen while we sing to you.*

Then fists began pounding on tabletops while the chant of "Come out! Come out!" echoed throughout the huge room.

In a few minutes, three women ranging in age from twenty-something to sixty stepped out of the kitchen and into the room, and the campers and counselors rose in respect, cheering. Heidi joined them and admired the three women who, for most of the summer, worked in relative obscurity in the confines of that hot kitchen.

Suddenly the light broke through Heidi's thick skull. It took more than just people in the spotlight to do the work of Christ. It took people willing to work in cramped quarters, to give without ever expecting to receive credit. All of those names in Matthew were important to Christ's genealogy but only a few names were famous. Even among the disciples, Thaddeus and Bartholomew were rarely mentioned, but that didn't make them any less important.

Her eyes swept the cafeteria. Two, three, maybe four of all the counselors she saw had risen to the top of the popularity list among the campers, but there was no way the camp would have been a success without the other twenty. The kitchen staff got a shout-out at the end of the week, but the maintenance crew would probably go unrecognized.

Camp was meant to provide an environment for discovery and growth for the young campers. Heidi smiled wanly. She didn't know if the young campers learned anything, but she knew one older one who had.

Follow the Rules

"There is no way I am wearing all this dorky gear," Samantha asserted.

"Then there's no way you will be working for me," the foreman of the work crew replied calmly.

Samantha's mouth dropped open as she stared incredulously at the foreman. "You've got to be kidding. You mean to say that if I refuse to wear this—this—" she stared at the bright orange lightweight jacket held distastefully between two fingers, "you're going to fire me?"

"That's right."

Samantha choked in disbelief and looked around at the others. "That's discrimination," she said haughtily.

"That's being smart," he countered. "And those are the rules." He held his hand out toward her. "Now if you don't want to be a part of this work crew, then why don't you hand me your jacket."

Samantha glanced around the group for some support, but mouths remained shut.

"Boy, you guys must need this job pretty bad," she said. "One reason I didn't take the job at Bucky Burgers was because of the ridiculous get-up they make you wear, but at least there you're comfortable. You guys are all going to die of heat exhaustion." She let the jacket drop from her two-finger hold, just out of reach of the foreman. "It's all yours," she said as she turned on her heel and left.

Keri watched her go, amazed at her brazenness. She would never dream of speaking to a boss like that, and she wondered why Samantha had even taken time to apply for a job with the Youth Work Crew.

Mr. Blackwell, the foreman, said nothing until Samantha was out of sight. Then he turned to those remaining. "Any others of you have reservations? If so, leave now." No one left. No one even moved. "All right then, gather your gear and go get ready. We'll meet back here in fifteen minutes."

The twenty remaining teenagers began gathering up their equipment. Keri reached for hers and, for a second, thought Samantha might have had a point. In ninety and a hundred degree heat, it seemed a bit much to have to wear heavy, calf-high work boots, a hard hat, a kerchief, long pants, and a bright orange jacket just to pick up litter and clear away debris from the roads and highway. In addition, Mr. Blackwell had stressed that under no circumstances was anyone to work alone, but always in twos and only in areas that were posted by temporary work signs. Also, each person had to lug along a large canteen of water. It all seemed like overkill, but those were the rules.

• • •

At ten o'clock, Mr. Blackwell honked the horn for a break, and Keri was already feeling the heat and was extremely thankful for the large canteen of water. She had emptied half of it already.

"Fill 'em up out of the jugs in the back of the truck," Mr. Blackwell instructed. "Then wet down your kerchiefs and place them under your hard hats."

"Can't we take our jackets off?" someone asked. Mr. Blackwell shook his head.

"Two reasons why," he said patiently. "One, cars have *got* to see you. People daydream when driving on freeways or roads they drive frequently. Even with the signs posting "work crews ahead," drivers aren't expecting to see you so close to the road. We want to make sure they do. And second, we can't afford to have you get a sunburn. Not only does it inhibit your work in subsequent days, but you then run the risk of skin cancer down the road. I realize that's not your concern right now, but it's ours.

"Now, let's get back to work. Mike, you and Glen are going to head over toward those fences there and hack away at those high weeds. Fire danger. Keri, you and Ben will take litter patrol beginning about a half mile up the road. Stuart …"

Mr. Blackwell divvied out the late morning assignments. Keri wet her kerchief, stuck it along the band of her hard hat, and then placed it back on her head.

"If this is supposed to keep the sun off of us, why don't they let us wear something a little more fashionable like a straw hat with a wide brim?" she asked Ben.

"These things," she said and knocked on her own helmet, "are definitely fashion inept."

Ben smiled. "Are you trying to sound like Samantha?"

Beneath the dirt already accumulating on her face and neck, Keri felt herself blush. "Sorry," she said with a grin.

A car went racing by them and both involuntarily turned away from it. Suddenly, Keri felt a violent *whack* on the back of her hard hat.

"AHHHH," she screamed in surprise. Ben turned toward her.

"Are you all right?" he asked as he rushed over.

"What was that?" Keri asked, holding her head.

Ben looked around, stooped over, and picked up something off the ground a few feet from her. He held up a steel nut.

"This," he said. "That car ran over it at just the right angle that it shot out like a bullet. You know, like when small rocks shoot out and crack your windshield. They don't have to be very big, but the velocity can do a lot of damage.

Keri took off her hard hat and looked at the where the

rock had made a huge dent in it. She placed it back on her head.

"Are you sure you're OK?" Ben asked.

Keri nodded. "I'm definitely going to have a headache, but at least I'm still alive. That thing could have killed me."

Ben nodded solemnly.

"Forget what I said about straw hats with nice brims," she continued with a wry grin. "I'll take ol' hard hat Harry here any day."

Keri was more than ready for lunch by the time twelve o'clock rolled around. She and Ben trudged back to the trucks, grabbed their lunches, and went to find some shade. Over a hundred feet from the roadway, she felt safe enough to finally take off her jacket.

I wouldn't do that if you're going to sit down there," Ben said watching her.

Keri looked up at him in surprise. "Why not?"

He pointed to a clump of three-leafed plants. "Poison oak," he whispered. "It's all over the place."

Keri's face contorted in misery. "Then where am I going to eat?"

"Either out in the sun without your jacket, or in the shade with it," Ben answered simply, "but don't stay out in the sun too long. Sunburn you know."

Keri sighed, pulled her jacket back on, and plopped down in a relatively uninfected portion of the grass.

"Did you hear what happened to Jim?" Mark asked. Ben and Keri shook their heads. "Rattlesnake bit him."

Keri's mouth dropped like a rock. "Is he OK? Did they have to cut him open and suck the venom out?" She was having flashbacks to health class and all the gory movies she had seen. Mark shook his head.

"Oh no. He's fine. Rattlers attack pretty low, and though it did penetrate his jeans, it hit the tops of his boots. I guess I shouldn't have said it bit him. It actually just attacked him. His boots saved him."

Keri felt a breath of relief rush from her. Every piece of clothing that she had silently, or openly, complained about had its purpose. They told drivers who they were and protected them from dangers they had no control over. Had she decided on her own to take off or change any one of them, or if Mr. Blackwell had relented even just a little because he felt sorry for them, she could either be battling a bad case of poison oak or, worse, be dead. So could Jim.

It may be socially acceptable to question and rebel against authority, assert your individuality, and demand your rights, she thought, *but, as long as what is being asked of you does not violate any of God's laws, it's wiser to follow the rules.*

Friends

Janet sat in the sixth pew from the back with the rest of her family. Every Sunday for as long as she could remember, they had sat there. Janet knew the back of every head in front of her and the singing voice of everyone behind her.

As the minister began the sermon, Janet mentally checked in and out, jotting down enough key phrases and references to keep her respectable during their family discussion at lunch. The rest of the time she daydreamed.

She glanced at her watch. Eleven-twenty. The service was dragging this morning. She pulled out her bulletin and started coloring in all the Os. Eleven-thirty. She went back and started on the Ps. The service finally ended at 11:45, and Janet breathed a sigh of relief. She was anxious to get on with her day.

Once home, she quickly changed and went out to help her mother with lunch. Tami, her little sister, was busy babbling about something, as usual, and Janet tried to ignore her.

"So do you think he'll do it, Mom? Huh? Do ya?" she asked anxiously. She was trying to stand still, but that's difficult for any twelve-year-old, let alone one bursting with excitement.

As much as Janet hated it, Tami's behavior roused her curiosity.

"Does Mom think who will do what?" she asked.

Tami turned toward her with a smug smile on her face. I'm going to write Jordan Knight of New Kids on the Block and ask him to donate $5,000 to help the homeless here in Lakewood," she said emphatically, her eyes gleaming.

Janet involuntarily laughed and gave Tami an incredulous look.

"He's *not* going to send money here," she said emphatically. "He doesn't even *know* you!"

"We're good friends," Tami retorted, pulling her lip into a thin, tight line and crossing her arms defiantly. "I know all about him."

Janet shook her head. "Come off it, Tami. You don't even know the guy."

"He was born on May 17, 1971. He has brown hair and dark brown eyes. He's 5' 10" and weighs 155 pounds. He has five brothers and sisters, his middle name is Nathaniel, and he likes ketchup on everything!" she said all in one breath.

Janet just laughed. "You got all that out of some teen magazine. That doesn't make him your friend. You haven't even met him."

"I went to his concert," she countered.

"Ooh, that'll do it," Janet taunted. "Tami," she said seriously. "You have to spend time with people before you can be their friend. You have to get to know what they're thinking. Confide in them. Share your feelings with them."

Tami could take no more. She turned and stomped out of the room, but before the bedroom door slammed shut they heard, "I'm still going to write him that letter!" BANG!

"Kids," Janet said shaking her head sadly. Her mother watched her.

"There might have been a better way to let her down," suggested Mrs. Gerry. Janet disagreed.

"She would only get her hopes up that Jordan Knight would actually answer her request, Mom, and she doesn't even know him. You and I both know there's no way he's sending money."

Her mother said not more.

• • •

Sunday afternoon went by quickly as it always did, and the Gerrys went to the evening service at six. When they returned, Janet went to her room to run through her prayer list. Like clockwork, every Sunday evening at seven-thirty sharp, she was at her desk praying. Sometimes, if the list was long, she had trouble concentrating and would drift off, not paying attention to what she was saying.

She closed her bedroom door and looked for her Bible. It wasn't on her desk.

"I must've left it out on the counter," she mumbled and went to the kitchen to get it. Sure enough, there it was. She reached for it, then stopped. Lying right next to it was the envelope, sealed and stamped, and neatly addressed to Jordan Nathanial Knight.

Janet shook her head and laughed. *Whatever*, she thought.

She went back to her room, closed the door, sat down at her desk, and pulled out the list.

Great, she thought. *A long one.* She knew most of the people on it, but felt little concern for their situations. Still it was her Christian duty to pray for them. She started at the top, but before she was even to number two, her mind had wandered to her words to Tami about her letter.

He won't answer. You don't even know him. A sharp pain surged through her and she swallowed hard.

You got all that from some teen magazine. Janet began to feel warm, and tiny beads of sweat formed on her forehead. More of her words echoed in her mind.

You have to spend time with someone. Know what they're thinking. Share your feelings ....

Janet stopped. One of the tiny beads was rolling down her face and her palms felt sticky. She looked down at the prayer list, then at her Bible, and then at the small picture of Christ hanging over her bed. She stared at the picture a long time, as though trying to pull some hidden meaning or feeling out of it, but it was no use.

"Might as well be looking at a picture of Jordan Knight in a magazine," she said sadly. "I don't even know Him. Why *should* He answer my prayers?"

She sighed deeply. She was no better than Tami. She called herself a Christian, but she didn't even *know* Christ. She'd read all about Him, knew all the vital statistics—the facts—but she couldn't call Him a friend. She had never spent time getting to know Him, confiding in Him, and most of all relying on Him.

"Tami's got me beat there," she said. "At least she's *looking* for an answer. I don't even care enough to do that."

She thought about church that morning and coloring in the Os and Ps and suddenly she felt extremely embarrassed. *That's like going to a concert, sitting in the front row, and then doing a crossword puzzle all evening. How rude.*

She sat quietly in her chair, the prayer list forgotten. She pulled her Bible toward her, gingerly fingering the leather binding. She had read the verses and gathered the information, but she hadn't actually spent time with Him. How did that work exactly?

Like any other friend, she heard an inaudible voice say. *Let's just talk.*

Janet opened her Bible to John and went straight for the

red letters, Jesus's own words. She would let Him talk first while she listened and thought. Then she would respond.

Gifts

"Good-bye, Niki! See you tonight for dinner! Have a good day with Grandma!" Niki's mother yelled on her way out the door to the garage.

Niki cringed. "Geez," she mumbled under her breath. "Do you think you could yell it a little louder?" And then she held her breath and listened, hoping, praying, that her mother's overzealous good-bye hadn't awakened her grandmother.

"Niki? Are you out there?"

Niki released the pent-up air inside her with a vengeance. *Well, that's just fine,* she thought. *Thanks a lot Mom. I might have had another hour to myself, a half hour at least, but noooo, you had to make sure Grandma was good and awake so I could earn my pay.*

She thought about not answering, but her conscience, always a major thorn in her side, got to her right away.

"Yeah, Grandma, I'm here!" she yelled, trying to sound cheerful enough, but knowing her words came out laced with exasperation. She stayed on the couch and waited. Nothing. Finally, from down the hall came a feeble response.

"Can I get you to help me?" her grandmother called.

Niki tossed her book on the couch, stood up, and scolded herself. "I knew she wanted me," she mumbled to herself. "I didn't need to make her beg. After all, I am getting paid for it."

That was another part of the problem. Taking care of her grandmother was her summer job, from seven to five every day. And her mother was paying her pretty well, too. Ten bucks an hour. But the problem was she had no choice. Had she been asked, she would have declined and looked for work at the rec department instead of being stuck in her house all day long with a feeble octogenarian. Everyone else was using their gifts, their talents, like they had talked about in Sunday school a few weeks ago. Stephanie was giving piano lessons, Jason was building houses with his dad, Renee and Paul were lifeguards.

She had planned on refereeing volleyball and softball games and being a counselor at the city sports day camps. She was a talented athlete and loved athletics. So what was *she* doing this summer? Wasting away babysitting her eighty-plus-year-old grandmother.

She arrived at the guest room to find her grandmother caught in the folds of her sheets—half in bed and half out. How long she had been like that Niki wasn't sure. As she hustled over to help, she felt her conscience prick again.

"Grandma, are you okay?" she asked as she helped the older woman untangle herself.

"Oh, I'm fine," she said. "Just not as young as I used to be and can't get my feet working like they should."

"You're not old, Grandma," Niki countered. "And you get around really well."

Grandma shook her head. "I used to be able to beat the boys at basketball. Don't think I could do that now," she chuckled. Niki laughed too. Her mom had said that Niki had inherited her athletic abilities from her grandmother. Too bad she hadn't inherited her good sense of humor too.

"Would you like me to get your clothes for you?" she asked.

"That would be nice," her grandmother replied, "but I was also wondering if you might help me wash my hair first, and then maybe style it for me. I haven't had my hair washed for a week."

Niki consented and helped her grandmother out to the kitchen sink, made sure she was stable, then ducked her head under the faucet and commenced to shampooing her head, thinking back to all the times her own mother had washed her hair this way when she was little. From somewhere under the suds she heard her grandmother.

"You have such nice, soothing hands," she said. "This feels so nice. Thank you."

"You're welcome," Niki said, not able to keep from smiling.

She rinsed her off, sat her on a chair, pulled out the hair dryer, and started styling.

"There!" Niki said triumphantly fifteen minutes later and held up a hand mirror. "What do you think?"

Grandma checked herself out from all angles. "I think that's the best I've looked in years," she said, and Niki laughed.

"Oh, Grandma," she scolded. "You're a beautiful lady. Why you have better looking legs than most twenty-year-olds."

Her grandmother looked down at her ankles that were slim and smooth and indeed much shapelier than some women decades younger than she.

"Your grandfather always liked my legs," she said.

Niki felt her herself blush to hear her grandmother talk like that.

"I sure do miss him," she added, and Niki felt herself shiver involuntarily. Her grandfather had died three years earlier, and Grandma had done all right on her own, but when she had fallen and almost broken her hip, Niki's mother and uncle became concerned. Niki's parents lived in the same town as her grandmother, so Grandma would live with them. Grandma protested loudly, saying she was fine, and had no intention on being a burden to any of her kids, but the kids won. Niki felt sorry for her. All her privacy and independence were gone, and now, she was having trouble even taking care of herself.

"What would you like to do today?" Niki asked, hoping to change the subject.

"Oh, if you wouldn't mind walking with me, I think I'd like to get out a little. I go a little stir crazy in here."

Me too, thought Niki.

They had a nutritious breakfast of Choco-Choco Krisps, Grandma's favorite. Then Grandma found her walker and the two headed out the door. Niki took a deep breath of early summer.

"Summer just smells different than the other seasons," she said without thinking.

"Um hum," agreed her grandmother. "It smells of maturity. You can smell the leaves, the grass, the weeds, even the dirt."

Niki had to agree. Grandma had a pretty good handle on it.

"Which season do you like best, Grandma?" she asked as they walked slowly down the street.

"I like them all," her grandmother said. "God has made each one so unique." she paused a moment. "Thank you for walking with me. You are so patient. I know you would like to walk faster. You have such young, strong legs. I'm sorry I can't get around as well as I used to."

Or as much as you'd like to, thought Niki sadly, though she had never heard her grandmother complain.

The two walked slowly through their neighborhood, which was adjacent to downtown, Niki listening as

Grandma told stories about who used to lived in all the houses, and what happened to that store, and how many businesses were ruined in the flood of '46. She listened enough to make an occasional comment now and then, but the distant sound of whistles and laughter from the city park brought back another pang of regret and a reminder that a whole summer would slip by without enjoying her passion and developing her God-given gifts.

"I think I'm read to go home now," her grandmother said, and Niki helped her grandmother turn her walker around. There would be no complaint from her.

The walk had tired Grandma, and she napped until about eleven and then turned on her favorite game show, trying to guess the phrase before the contestants. Niki fixed lunch and did the dishes while Grandma commented on how nice it was to be young and able to move around so well.

After lunch, Niki pulled out the book Grandma had wanted to read and opened it to the second chapter.

"My eyes tire easily," Grandma said. "Would you mind reading to me?" Niki had obliged. It was a pretty good book anyway.

"I need to write Charles," she said after Niki had finished reading. Charles was her son, Niki's uncle. "My handwriting's so bad though. Do you think you could write down what I say, Niki? You have such pretty handwriting." Grandma wasn't about to admit her arthritis was acting up again.

Niki pulled out a piece of stationary and wrote as her grandmother dictated the letter. It wasn't very long and didn't take much time at all.

"Well, I think I'll go lie down for a little while and get a bit more rest. Give you a little time for yourself, too," her grandmother said and struggled to get up out of the rocker. Niki started to protest and move to help but stopped. Her grandmother hadn't asked for her assistance this time and had her full concentration on the task at hand. Niki watched for what seemed like a long minute as the elderly lady rocked back and forth until she had gathered enough momentum to get up, grasp her walker firmly with both hands, and slowly maneuver it toward the little room in the back of the house that was now her home.

Niki watched her go and then sat back on the couch thinking. Sure she didn't have the summer job she coveted, refereeing games and coaching little kids, but she had been wrong to complain and think she was wasting her time and her talents. Youth, strength, eyesight. These were all gifts God had given her to share with a wonderful woman who was losing all of them because of age.

Gifts weren't always obvious. They came wrapped in many different ways and had to be opened to be discovered. She smiled. Perhaps this was the summer of discovering a few more of hers.

I am Bryan's Brain

"*Love the Lord your God with all your heart and with all your soul and with all your mind and with all your strength.*" *Mark 12:30.*

Please take note of the third portion of this verse because it applies to me. I am a brain. Bryan Bartok's brain to be exact. But that part really doesn't matter. I have been asked to represent all brains today to plead our case with all of you so-called "thinkers."

Not only do we believe that some of you take us for granted, but a lot of you don't even know us for who we truly are. We also have a bone to pick with the guy who wrote the commercial that showed a raw egg and then went, "This is your brain. This is your brain on drugs [into the ol' frying pan we go]. Any questions?" Man, talk about selling us down the river. Now most people think we're about as complicated as breakfast food.

Then there are some of you who aren't heeding the verse, "With *all* your mind." You give credit to the heart for having four parts and realize the rest of the circulatory system consists of veins, arteries, corpuscles, platelets, and such. You credit the digestive system with an esophagus, stomach, small and large intestine, etc. Even the pulmonary system gets divided into a couple of lungs, a trachea, a few alveoli and whatnot. Sure, but when you get to the ol' nervous system what do you say? A spinal cord and a brain. Talk about simplicity.

You *do* realize that we have our own little division of duties too, don't you? And if you didn't, well, that explains why some of you are a little weak in the ol' faith department.

Let me help you get back on track by educating you a bit. First of all, I can be divided into five parts. First, there is the lower brain (which takes care of all the menial chores like breathing, heartbeat, and so forth). On top of that is the limbic structure. It takes care of behavioral patterns such as sociability, hospitality, sexuality, aggression. Then the neocortex, where I'm speaking from, is divided into two halves connected by a bundle of nerve fibers call the *corpus callosum*.

Actually, if the truth be known, only the left side of me is speaking. The right side is mute. Now that doesn't mean it doesn't work or have any responsibilities. It's the side that has to manipulate abstract forms and three dimensional images, interpret rhythm, pitch, mood, and style, and deal with all those emotional cues. (And let me tell you, Bryan's right side here has a full day's work just trying to pick up on his girlfriend Katie's subtle messages.)

The left side is the one that gets all the credit, however, 'cause it's the side that deals with language, speech, reason, and a sense of self. It also had the dubious distinction of being known for its self-deception and rationalization. Pretty scary, isn't it?

Now the two sides get to talk back and forth to each other through the *corpus callosum,* which brings me back to my main gripe. A lot of you guys are just ignoring what my right side is trying to say with that ol' left brain self-deception.

Let me explain. Some of you Christians out there, and almost all of those non-Christians, have a lot of trouble dealing with the faith issue. You want everything in black and white, all your little ducks in a row. If you can't see it, you don't want to believe it. Well, let me tell you. That's your left brain talking. Nice little "everything in order," "make a list" left brain.

Do you know what the right side likes to go on? Intuition. (Bryan, like most guys, likes to call it a "gut feeling." Intuition is for girls, he claims.) That's right. While the left side must have all the facts and nothing but the facts, the right side doesn't care squat about facts. On a hunch, it can give you the whole picture, just not all the steps to that picture.

So what does this have to do with us Christians and faith? Look at Romans 1:20: *"For since the creation of the world God's invisible qualities—his eternal power and divine nature—have been clearly seen, being understood from what has been made, so that people are without excuse."* If you look around at the world and how it all interacts and works, if you just look at the complexity of your own body and how it works and mends itself, then you should get the whole picture even if you don't see each little step. There is a God!

This is all pretty heady stuff, isn't it? (Get it? Heady? Never mind.) But it is complicated. It has to be because we live in a complicated world.

Now, you should be asking yourself this question. Why did God, in His infinite wisdom, feel it necessary to divide the brain in half and give each a separate, almost conflicting function?

I, as a brain, can answer that for you. He did it because you need the ability to mix fact with faith and to incorporate reason with intuition. That's the way the world works according to God's laws, so that's the way the brain works. To know God you must use "*all* your mind."

Then why, you might ask, did He make almost ninety-five percent of the people left-brain dominant, so that the majority of people would really have to fight with themselves to have faith, to overcome that rationalization and accept a little bit of the right's "gut feeling?" Sorry, but I can't answer that one. I mean, I'm the clay, remember? I'm good, I'm smart, but I'm not better or smarter than the potter.

Anyway, let's sum up this entire discussion. I am *not* an egg. And though the whole human body is a complex structure, none of it would even function without me. So give me a little credit when it comes to figuring out that world out there. I'm ready. I'm up to the task. Just remember—use "*all* your mind!"

Line Call

Jerry carefully slid the post on and then shook his head to make sure the earring was secure. It dangled comfortably and he smiled. He then ran his fingers randomly through his shoulder-length hair, separating the thick strands before holding it in place with a headband. He stood up, adjusted his black power-liners and admired his new Nike tennis wear—black with flashes of hot pink. He picked up his rackets and bounced one off the strings of the other, testing their tension.

He grinned inwardly. If anyone were to see him now, from a distance, they would surely think they were looking at Andre Agassi. The thought brought a surge of adrenaline.

"Gentlemen, please take the court."

The umpire's directive broke Jerry from his thoughts. Quickly he bowed his head in full view of the crowd and prayed before discarding one racket and taking his position on the north end of the court.

The umpire was one of the luxuries of being in the finals

of the city championships. In all the other matches, the players kept their own scores and called their own lines. But in the finals, the umpire kept the score. Even though the players would still call their own lines, the umpire would overrule any blatant error and make a judgment call on any questionable call. It was the closest Jerry had ever been to a professional setting, and he relished it.

He warmed up smoothly, his strong, stocky body stroking the ball easily. Even to watch him hit that powerful forehand and that deceptive, two-handed backhand was to remind one of a young Agassi. And that was fine with Jerry. More than anything else, he wanted to play and look like the great tennis player.

Today was his first chance to break into the next echelon of his own tennis world. Across the net stood Robert Steiner, the defending champion of the sixteen-and-under division and the current valley champion. Though Jerry had upset some formidable players to earn the right to be in the finals, to beat Robert would solidify his rise to the top. He felt good, his muscles loose and ready. The umpire called the warmup to a halt.

"Gentlemen, begin play."

Jerry had won the toss and elected to serve. He held up two balls signaling he was ready. Robert nodded and positioned himself for the return. Jerry pushed some of the loose strands out of his eyes and then bounced the ball slowly in front of him, focusing himself on the point at hand. He looked across at Robert's position, readied himself, and then lifted the ball high above his left shoulder and into the court. A second later, his racket flashed through the air and the match was on.

For over an hour, the two battled away—slicing, hitting topspins, running, attacking, lobbing. Jerry had never played better tennis in his life, and he was on a high. Neither player could break the other's serve, and at 6-all, the umpire announced a tiebreaker.

Jerry served and won the first point then positioned himself for the return. Playing it safe, Robert served down the middle to Jerry's forehand and followed it in. Jerry had anticipated the shot and stepped in quickly, picking the ball up on the rise and then lashing it back crosscourt, catching Robert leaning the wrong way. It was a perfect passing shot and the mini-break he needed. With that one point advantage, he was able to hang onto his serves and win the first set 7-6.

The second set was just as grueling, and as the sun rose higher in the sky, Jerry's long hair became limp with sweat and clung uncomfortably to the back of his neck. His shirt was soaked and he felt himself tiring. He had never played such an exhausting match in his life. As he guzzled water, he glanced at Robert on the changeover and noticed the flush of his cheeks and the strain in his eyes.

The match is taking its toll on him, too, thought Jerry. *If*

I can just hang in there.

The two continued to hold serve and at four games to five, Jerry was serving to pull back even. The sun was unbearable now, shining right where his ball toss was and almost blinding him. He struggled for each point, but found himself down 30-40—break point, and set point for Robert. Jerry's feet felt like lead and his arms like sacks of flour. If he lost this point, he didn't think he would be able to muster enough strength and energy to pull out a third set.

He carefully took aim, noting that Robert had slid slightly to his right, leaving the backhand side of the court open and vulnerable. Jerry tossed the ball and smashed it to that side and followed his serve in to the net. Robert tried to recover and was only able to put his racket on the ball, but in doing so, he popped up a defensive lob that carried deep cross court.

Surprised, Jerry was caught flatfooted momentarily and then turned and raced after the ball. He knew before he got there that he would never make it and prayed the ball would be long. From many angles, the ball *did* look long. But from where Jerry was, the ball had definitely hit the line.

Immediately the internal battle began. He had to win this set; if he didn't then the match was as good as lost. He didn't have the energy to pull out the third set. If he called the ball out, he still had a chance.

But you're a Christian, stated his conscience. *You can't cheat. You can't call it out.*

But it was a fluke shot, he argued. *Robert never should have returned the ball. The point is rightfully mine.*

The argument was over in less than a second, and before the ball had a chance to bounce again, Jerry's hand was raised, signaling the ball long.

"Out!" he yelled.

"What?" yelled Robert, looking incredulously at the umpire. "That ball hit the line!"

A low murmur came from those watching. Jerry grew even hotter. He knew some had clearly seen the ball as he had, while others were too far out of position to know. Instinctively, all eyes turned toward the umpire, waiting to hear his ruling.

"I'm afraid Mr. Benton, as he was running back to play the ball, blocked my view. I can't make a call. We'll have to go with his word that the ball was out."

Robert jerked his head toward Jerry and just stared, waiting for him to reverse his call. Jerry tried to return the angry gaze but couldn't and turned to go back and serve. Robert stood in the center of the court, dejected and disbelieving. Finally, he moved back to receive Jerry's serve, but the fight seemed to be gone. He too was exhausted. The set had been his. Though he was still a game up, and the score even, it seemed too much now. His fight was gone.

Jerry won the next two points and then the next two games to win the set and the match.

The awards presentation took place right after the match. Jerry was handed the two-foot trophy and asked to pose for the papers. He quickly removed his headband and swept his hair back out of his face.

"C'mon, smile," said one photographer. "You should be happy. You won!"

Jerry complied, but inside he didn't feel like smiling. The guy was right; he should be happy. He should be thrilled! Then why wasn't he? He had just beaten the defending champion. He shoved the niggling reminder of that crucial point into the back of his mind. It was only *one* point. Robert didn't *have* to fold. He could have still won. It was *his* choice to give up. But even those thoughts didn't give him much peace, and he tried a different tack.

Tennis was important to him. Possibly his future. *More important than God?* a voice whispered.

Robert's shot was a fluke, he told himself. *He didn't deserve the point.*

So you are justified in calling it out? In lying? came that irritating inner voice.

Jerry kept the smile for the reporters plastered on his face while the voices fought it out it within him.

You cannot serve God and mammon.

He wasn't sure which voice had said that, but it hit home hard. Jerry stared at the gold trophy grimly. The gold glittered in the afternoon sunlight, but from his perspective it already looked a little tarnished. The victory he had thought about all week was now hollow, tainted, and unsavory. He could plainly see that when he had called that ball out, he had made his choice, and it was not for God.

More than Muscle

Eric leaned back in his chair and scrutinized the scene before him, starting from the levee at his left then sweeping his eyes to his right as far as he could see.

The beach was saturated with people. Some hadn't moved since they had arrived earlier that morning. Others, kids mostly, had never been still. Then there were those in the ocean itself. Surfers, body surfers, boogie boarders, swimmers, waders, all trying to share the same space. It was a recipe for disaster, and it was Eric's job to make sure disaster didn't happen.

He adjusted his umbrella and then his sunglasses and brushed off a minute piece of sand from his bright red swim trunks.

"Hi, Eric!"

He glanced up in time to see Katie and Sheryl strolling casually by beneath him. Katie waved coyly. Eric grinned and subtly flexed a bit to show off his muscles. The girls smiled and walked by. He felt himself tingle all over.

Definitely one of the perks of this job. The girls were all over you. Lifeguards were grade A meat, and he didn't mind that one bit.

He checked himself over. He could hold his own. He was tanned to a deep bronze. His stomach was tight and had that washboard ripple. His shoulders were broad, his hips thin, and his legs and arms muscular. The sun had also bleached out his light brown hair giving it that surfer look. Yup, if he had to say so himself, he could carry his own with the girls.

"Gonna save another life, Eric?"

This time it was Patty.

"If I have to," he said seriously and puffed up a bit. That was another reason he was getting so much attention today. He had saved someone yesterday—well technically. Some guy got a cramp in his calf and was going under, and Eric had grabbed the life buoy and ran into the water to get him. The guy could have just stood up, it wasn't that deep, but he had panicked. So now everyone he knew thought he had saved the guy's life. And who was he to burst their bubble. Anyway had the guy *actually* been drowning, he could have done it. In order to get this job, he had to be able to swim three miles in the ocean and prove his life-saving skills.

He moved his umbrella, stretched out his legs, and surveyed his territory again. *A lot of people out today,* he mused and tried to see how many people he could pick out that he knew. He was to ten when he heard the scream.

"HELP! HELP!"

Eric looked toward the water but couldn't see anything. Suddenly, it seemed like the whole beach was moving with people scurrying toward the water. Eric tried to locate the cries. "Please help! My boy! He's drowning!"

Someone rushed up to his stand.

"Over there!" the guy shouted, pointing about a hundred years down the beach. Eric could now see the frantic mother, and he grabbed his life buoy, jumped to the sand, and ran at a full sprint. When he got there, she was pointing toward a spot in the ocean.

"He's out there," she cried, and Eric tried to pick up something, some clue as to where the child might be.

"How old is he?" he asked quickly.

"Eight," she cried. "One minute he was on this side of the waves, and then the next, he was on the other. I don't know how it happened."

Eric ran into the surf. *Eight is so small,* he thought. He could waste time mentally berating the mother who let her son venture too far out or focus his energy on finding him. He scanned the horizon. Nothing.

Various swimmers were pointing at different spots, but none of them agreed.

"Please, Lord," he prayed as he threw the life buoy over his shoulder and dove into the water. "Please help me find him."

He couldn't open his eyes to look around; he could only feel. His ability to swim three miles, run two, and administer CPR were useless in the current situation. Without knowing exactly where the boy had disappeared, it would be like looking for the proverbial needle in the haystack. And a needle that kept moving.

Lord, please bring him to me, he prayed. *There's no way I can find him on my own.*

He swam to where he thought the mother had pointed, then tread water and looked around. Nothing broke the surface. He took a deep breath and submerged, feeling around him, trying to locate the boy. He stayed under until his lungs hurt, and then he came up for air and looked around again. From the beach, the mother was going into hysterics. He took another huge breath.

This time, Lord. It's got to be this time. The boy had been under for almost three minutes. He had to find him soon. He felt something brush against his leg and quickly reached for it, but it was only a piece of kelp. He couldn't stay under any longer and again came up for air.

He was now beginning to panic himself. Why hadn't he paid closer attention? While he was busy patting himself on the back and admiring his own physique, this kid was going into water he had no business being in.

He tried to calm himself and looked across the surface of the ocean for something—anything. *Please, Lord. Save him. Don't let him pay for my selfish inattention.*

And then he saw it. Almost twenty yards away, a little piece of yellow rubber, like from a mask or a swim fin.

He powered his way to it and grabbed beneath the surface of the water. A leg. He dove under and pulled the small figure to him and then surfaced.

He could tell instantly that the boy was not breathing. He tucked his arm around him and swam toward shore, thankful that the tide was with him.

Once on shore, he laid the small figure on the ground, checked his mouth for blockage, and then began to administer CPR, all the while praying as the boy's mother cried over his shoulder.

Please save him, Lord. Don't take him now after you led me to him. Not now.

He pumped on the little chest four times and then blew in another breath then pumped another four times. He could hear the ambulance siren in the distance, getting closer and closer.

Come on. Come on. Finally a sputter, and then a cough, and Eric quickly turned the small head to the side as salt water made its way back out. Eric felt himself relax and then tremble slightly.

"Back up," he directed. "Let's give him some room."

The crowd obeyed as the mother dropped to her knees and stroked the boy's forehead through her tears.

"Here come the paramedics!" someone shouted and the crowd parted like the Red Sea to let the medics through.

They dropped down next to the boy and began checking his vitals.

"Looks like he'll be all right," said one, "but let's get him to the hospital anyway to make sure." He looked at Eric. "Good job. You saved this boy's life."

Eric shook his head. He had learned his lesson. He hadn't saved this life. There was no way he would have found that boy out in that ocean, and he knew it.

"I'm afraid I can't take credit for this," he said, his voice still a little shaky. "It was a miracle I even located him. God saved his life, not me."

New Girl

Carin and I race-walked as fast as we could to the front of the church and slid down the first pew until we bumped into Tommy Davidson. We bottled up like bumper cars and then giggled. None of it was very sacred for a worship service, but we didn't really think about that. After all, we were displaying our enthusiasm for our church youth group.

I mean, look at us. We always sat together and always filled up at least the first three rows, right in front of Pastor Kent. He would always smile down on us, and we would always pretend to pay close attention to what he was saying by jotting down notes and such.

During the singing, we would sometimes all sway back and forth in unison and even lead the congregation in a few of the newer songs. We were tight and involved. In essence, at least in our eyes, we were an exemplar youth group, and we loved it.

Carin and I slid back over a tad to give Tommy a little more space.

"Save some room for Kristen," Carin said. "She has to collect money for summer camp."

I slid over even more and set my Bible down next to me, possessively warning off others who might want to sit there. I turned around and watched others in the youth group working their way up the aisles, two by two, laughing and giggling and just enjoying each other's company. Music played over the sound system while the church filled, and I sang the words silently.

And they'll know we are Christians by our love, by our love.

And they'll know we are Christians by our love.

That was definitely us.

"Where's Ben?" I asked, turning around again to scan the church. We always looked out for each other.

"I think he's talking to Pastor Jerry about special music for next Sunday evening's service," Carin answered.

On my second sweep of the sanctuary, I saw her. A new girl. She was sitting toward the back on the opposite side with what looked like her parents. My eye stopped ever so slightly and then kept going. I didn't want her to know I had seen her. I turned around and felt my skin crawl.

I knew we were supposed to encourage new teens to join us, but they always caused a momentary rift in the unity. They didn't know us, and we didn't know them, and it just made for an all-around awkwardness, especially if you were the one to discover them. Because, suddenly, you had to be their caretaker. And if it turned out you really didn't like them, then you were still stuck, 'cause you were the first person they had met. It just wasn't a good deal any way you looked at it. I turned back around for good and started chatting with Carin.

• • •

Sithong watched as the teenagers worked their way down the aisle and then crowded into the first three pews. She watched them giggle and laugh and talk and wave each other over. They seemed to enjoy each other so much. Her own heart ached for that companionship.

Being new in town was hard enough, but being new in a church was even harder, harder even than high school, because the teen pool was smaller. People already knew each other so well. She prayed silently that maybe one of the youth group might look her way and smile or come and say hi, but they all seemed pretty preoccupied. One girl did look back, and Sithong thought she might have seen her, but just as she was starting to smile back at her, the girl's eyes had moved on, and then she had turned back around.

Sithong felt that deep loneliness in her chest again. The other girl must have just been looking for someone.

• • •

The service was getting reading to start and now we were

all turning around looking for latecomers. I made sure I kept my eyes on my own side of the sanctuary. I didn't want to risk making eye contact with the new girl. If I did, I knew I'd just have to say something after the service, just to be polite. And she looked, I don't know, Korean or something like that, and I wasn't sure if we'd have anything in common or even if she could speak English. By the time the service started, I had a pretty good list of reasons why I shouldn't introduce myself.

• • •

A couple sat in front of Sithong and her parents and turned around to introduce themselves. Her parents' faces brightened and the four of them chatted pleasantly for a few minutes. SIthong kept watching the front three rows, hoping someone might see her. They all kept turning, kept waving, but not at her. Perhaps she should go up there, make the effort to introduce herself. But before she could work up the courage, the service started.

• • •

The pastor's sermon wasn't all that exciting, so we just passed notes back and forth planning our strategy for camp.

We should each invite someone from school, Carin wrote. *We did that last year and a few came.* Multiple yeses were written in the margin by the time it came around to me.

We should have a time of cabin sharing and then whole camp sharing, Aaron had suggested. More yeses. I passed the note on.

I should have been more involved in one of the activities taking place, the sermon or the note passing, but something was working on me, and I had this uneasy feeling that it was God. Suddenly our tight little group of active teenage Christians was looking more and more like a little clique of blind Pharisees. We liked all the show, and we liked the comfort of the group, and we liked the way we did things, the ol' status quo, but we weren't too eager to step out and take a chance.

I thought about the two suggestions that had passed by. Most of them had asked friends they knew would say yes or who wouldn't be offended if they were asked. And as for the time of sharing? Well, let's just say, in the past, most of the sharing was about others, not too much self-revelation.

I adjusted myself, uncomfortable in all sorts of ways, and thought perhaps I should start listening to the sermon, but my conversation with myself had lasted a bit too long. The sermon was over.

• • •

Sithong let her eyes fall from the huge screen where the words of the song had been displayed and bowed her head for the closing prayer. While every other bowed head was probably following the pastor's prayer, she was praying her own.

Please, Lord, just let one *person say hello. Just* one.

Her need for Christian teen fellowship was intense.

The "amen" sounded and the congregation was dismissed to the sound of more piped music. Sithong followed her parents out the door and into the foyer, realizing now that the responsibility lay on her, so she searched for one person to introduce herself to.

As the teenagers shuffled toward her, laughing and talking, she kept her head up and stayed alert, waiting to make eye contact and move forward, but no one seemed to even notice her.

She let out a sigh of disappointment. Maybe next week.

"Hello."

Sithong turned around and there *I* stood—very nervous—but the smile on her face and in her eyes made all my nervousness disappear.

"You're new here, aren't you?" I asked.

"Yes, we just moved up from Fresno," she said and seemed anxious to talk.

I breathed a sigh of relief. She spoke English.

"Well, my name is Jill," I said extending my hand.

"I'm Sithong," she replied as she took my hand and shook it with gratitude.

"That's an interesting name," I said.

"It's Laotian."

My eyebrows rose. "Laotian?" Did you ever live in Laos?"

Sithong nodded. "It's where I became a Christian."

My eyes grew wider, my interest piqued, and my fears forgotten.

"Gee, you'll have to share that with the high school group. We're having a summer camp in two weeks. It would be a great chance to really get to know all of us and for us to get to know you."

We kept talking as we walked out to the parking lot, and she was so interesting that I forgot all about Carin and Ben and Aaron and ….

Pressure

"Do you mind if we talk?" my mom asked, sticking her head around my bedroom door.

I was right in the middle of a chemistry term paper and had my bed littered with papers holding important pieces of data. Since there really wasn't any method to my madness at this point, I merely shuffled an armload out of the way and nodded toward the space now available.

She came in and sat down on the edge, I think a little afraid that if she made herself *too* comfortable, she might be attacked by the leftover papers still scattered about.

She looked a little tired. I glanced at my clock. Eight-thirty. It wasn't *that* late. That could only mean one thing. This talk was going to be one of the heavy duty ones. We'd already had the "birds and the bees" talk, and the drug talk, so I wasn't sure what this one might be.

She gave me a weak smile.

"It's not easy being a teenager these days," she began, and I felt my head give a little involuntary jerk. That was an interesting statement coming from a woman who had grown up in the sixties.

"Oh, I don't know, Mom," I answered, trying to put her at ease. "Your teen years didn't seem like they were too easy."

She gave a little laugh and relaxed.

"I guess you're right," she answered. "The drug revolution, the sexual revolution, Viet Nam, protests." She shook her head and smiled. "Maybe you don't have it so rough."

I laughed. We both knew that wasn't true.

She readjusted herself on the bed and a pile of papers made a move toward her. I think I saw her shudder.

"I wanted to talk to you about this Friday night," she began, and I froze. This weekend was my first date—in my life. My parents were of the "old school" (or perhaps it was because of their growing up in the sixties) that said you shouldn't date until you were sixteen. We had had more than just a few heated discussions over that little rule; we had had some major battles.

I was young for my class so hadn't turned sixteen until this fall—my junior year. Now I was bound and determined to make up for lost time. My instincts warned me to be wary. Nothing good could come out of this conversation.

"What about Friday night?" I asked cautiously. Danny Beattie was not going to be stood up if that's what she had in mind.

I guess she could read my thoughts through the tone of

my voice (not really that difficult) because she smiled and shook her head.

"Don't worry," she said. "We're not taking your date away." I felt myself relax a little. "We just want you to be careful."

I felt my face grow red, so I threw my eyes toward the heavens in one of those "I can't believe we're having this conversation" looks.

"I will," I said with exasperation. "Don't you trust me?"

"I trust you," she said, "but I don't trust the world we're living in. I want you to go in with your eyes open."

"Danny's a Christian, too, Mom," I reminded her.

"I know," she said, "but sometimes that's not enough. A lot of people claim to be Christians for their own gain. Others who truly are Christians will often rationalize sinful behavior. While others, who truly do want to be obedient to God, fall to the pressure of the situation. They did in my day, and I know they do now."

I thought about this a little.

"Remember Paul said, and I paraphrase, what I want to do I don't do, but what I hate, I do. Plus as time goes on, people will be increasingly more lovers of themselves, unholy, lacking self-control."

I stared at her incredulously.

"Gee Mom, I'm only having one date, and you're making it seem like the end of the world!"

We both just looked at each other a moment and then

burst out laughing.

"That was pretty good, wasn't it?" I said, "because you *were* talking about the end of the world."

Mom shook her head, her laughter now reduced to a chuckle. "I'm sorry, I didn't mean to put a damper on your first date. Your father and I really do want you to have a wonderful time, but … well, we're your parents, and we worry about you and care for you.

"I know," I told her.

She nodded and stood up, really looking for the first time at the disaster on my bed.

"Speaking of final days," she said, and we both laughed as she walked to the door. "Good night."

The door closed, and I breathed out the sigh of relief reserved for these heavy meetings, but what Mom had said stuck with me. I reached for my Bible and turned to 2 Timothy and read the entire list that my mother had been referring to.

Every one of those attributes I saw daily and more than once. Some kids trading their youth for work in order to buy things they didn't need. Others spouting abusive and vulgar language, while others were bragging about how they had fooled their parents or complaining that their parents didn't buy them what they wanted. And then there were the boasts about sleeping with this guy or that girl but never about self-control.

I shivered involuntarily. Mom was right. This was

a tough time to be a teenager, but I couldn't become paranoid. Look at Mom. It wasn't an easy time to be a parent either. Everywhere one turned an anti-Christian message was flying in the face of a Christian parent's advice. TV glorified dysfunctional families and unbiblical behavior. Even some churches were twisting scripture to say that it was okay to love the sin as well as the sinner.

No, Mom was right on two counts: this was not an easy time to live, and I did need to be vigilant ... aware.

I closed my Bible and then my eyes, and I felt like I had on my first scuba dive. The further down I drifted, the greater the pressure on my ears and lungs. But that pressure was a reminder of my depth. A diver always used those little physical reminders to help gauge where he was. In diving I had learned to read the signs of danger and how to equalize the pressure in my ears and lungs.

Swimming through these adolescent years would be no different. There would be pressures but they should always remind me to equalize—to return to God's Word, to surround myself with accountability, to rely on my parents' wisdom—so that I could withstand the pressure and arrive at the surface safely.

I knew I was lucky to have parents who loved and cared for me so much that they had taught me biblical principles. Parents, who even now, when I most wanted my freedom, were willing (despite all my protests) to act as my regulator.

Read the Manual

"This camera is a piece of—" yelled Robert, and then added a few more expletives just to make sure his point was made. "I bet Mom and Dad got this second hand, and it's broken."

I winced at Robert's fourth pronouncement of the day that he always got the raw end of the deal, had the worst luck, received the rudest treatment ….

"But it was all sealed when you opened it," I countered.

"You can pay people to do that these days," Robert said with more sarcasm than was necessary.

I guess you could, but it sure seemed like a lot of trouble to me. I looked at the offending object Robert was tinkering with. It was a brand new (at least I thought it was brand new) Nikon F4. It was one of those cameras that the professionals used out in the field. It had more knobs and modes and numbers and computer chips than any camera or computer I had ever seen before. I wasn't even sure how to turn it on, and I'd taken photography last year.

"Maybe you should read the manual," I said innocently.

"Maybe you should just mind your own business," he shot back.

The remark smarted. I had only made a suggestion. He didn't need to jump all over me. I got up to leave. As much as I wanted to see how Robert's new camera worked, I didn't want to sit through another hour of abuse. It wasn't worth it.

"Where are you going?" he asked sharply.

"Out."

"Thought you wanted to see how the camera worked."

"Thought you said it was busted."

Robert ignored that remark. He always ignored questions he didn't have answers for or statements that called into question his own comments. I turned and walked out the door. Another good day gone bad. I slammed the door (accidentally, of course) and headed out to the living room where my parents were. I was mad. Robert had promised to take me up in the mountains to try out the new camera he had gotten for his birthday, and now that he was off on another one of his rampages, I knew we weren't going anywhere. I grabbed a throw pillow off the couch, wrapped my arms around it, then fell onto the couch and stared angrily at the television screen which was showing, of all things, golf! The day couldn't get much worse.

"What's the matter, Tyler?" my mother asked in that concerned tone that only mothers can muster.

"Nothing," I answered in that obnoxious, "I'm-not-going-to-tell-you-but-you-should-keep-on-asking" tone that only teenagers can produce.

"Seems like something," she pursued.

Whew! She hadn't believed me.

"Doesn't look like we'll be going up to Medicine Lake," I said flatly.

Her eyebrows shot up in surprise.

"Why not?" Dad asked, though his eyes never left the TV screen, which to me looked like a camera just panning blue sky. Suddenly, the camera dropped, and a puny little white ball bounced, then rolled on the grass. This was a stupid game to watch on TV.

"Robert can't get the camera to work," I replied, my answer tinged with impatience and bitterness.

Mom looked concerned. "Why not? Is is broken?"

I thought about telling her what he had said about them buying a used one, but the blue sky shots broke to commercial, and Dad jumped into the conversation.

"No, it's not broken. It's just pretty complicated. Is he reading the manual?" he asked.

I jumped on this like Shaquille O'Neal on an eight-foot basket, tossing the pillow aside.

"No. Can you believe it? He thinks he knows everything about everything, just because he's owned a camera before. If you ask me, I think he's gonna bust it."

Dad raised himself out of his chair. "I think I'd better

see what's going on," he said and disappeared down the hallway.

I slumped back in the the couch, grabbed another throw pillow and wrapped my arms around it, and thought I should be feeling better than this, having just ratted on my brother in a sense. But I didn't. The day was still ruined, and I was as frustrated as ever. Of all my family, and there were six of us in total, my brother was the only one I had a hard time getting along with. If the truth be known, I had a hard time liking him half of the time. Broken promises, yelling, swearing (even though he claimed to be a Christian), complaining about how the whole world was against him. He really wasn't a very likable guy, and I always seemed to be the *other* guy who wound up on the short end.

My blood was churning pretty good by now. I had to do something.

"I'm going out to shoot some baskets," I announced to anyone who might be listening and threw the pillow back on the couch. Now I knew how it got its name.

"Have fun," my mother said, now seeming oblivious to what was going on inside me.

I grabbed the basketball, dribbled a couple of times, and then heaved it toward the basket. I had about as much touch as a jackhammer on pavement, and the ball careened off the left side of the rim and headed for the street. I almost let out one of Robert's favorite words but caught myself. I ran after it, dribbled back up the driveway with more force than necessary and tried to calm myself. But the more I thought about Robert, the more I thought about all the other times he had ruined for me, and the madder I got. I stopped dribbling, went over to the big ash tree, and sat down on the basketball.

"God, what am I going to do?" I said aloud, not really sure if I was praying or just voicing my frustration … but just in case He was listening ….

Out of the blue came—no answer. I was used to that. I had been praying about Robert for over a year now: that God would change him, that God would make him see how selfish he was being, that God would make him a good Christian. And what did I get for a year of prayers? Nothing. Diddly squat. Well, that and a boatload of swear words and anger.

I took a deep breath. What was I going to do? Though it's not a good practice, I relived the scene that just had just taken place.

Why don't you read the manual? I had asked.

That hadn't been such a stupid remark. If he had, we would have been up at Medicine Lake by now taking photos. But no. He knew all there was to know about cameras because he had owned one before. Right. Like playing golf once made you and expert. Like—I stopped for a moment. *Like being a Christian meant you already knew all the answers?* I thought about that one for a moment.

Here I was all over Robert's case for not reading the manual, specifically designed to tell him how to work the camera, and I was doing pretty much the same thing with him. I knew the Bible was filled with stories about brothers who didn't get along—envious, jealous, cruel, spiteful, domineering, scornful brothers. How about ol' Cain and Abel for starters? Then Isaac and Ishmael, Jacob and Esau. Oh, and how about Joseph and his brothers? Look how long he had to wait for that to be resolved. More than just one year.

My blood began to churn again, but this time out of excitement not frustration. The Bible was *my* manual, and it was chock full of ways that these men of God either followed God's leading when dealing with their brothers … or didn't. How they prayed for their relationships and acted in a godly manner … or didn't.

I stood up and dribbled out to the foul line and took aim. Calmly, I lined up my shot and released the ball from my hand, letting it roll off my fingertips. It sailed through the air and then came down with a resounding *swish*!

I'd nailed it.

Something Stinks

"Wow! An RV! This is really cool!" Stacy said, beside herself. "Now we can go camping and not get all dirty and actually sleep in comfort. This is neat!"

Mr. Meyers let out a loud laugh, but Greg only glowered at her.

"You're *supposed* to get dirty camping," he growled. "Why else would you go?"

Shelly, Stacy's twin, curled her lip in a sly smile. "Please show us in the camping manuals where it says that in order to be truly camping you have to be grungy, grimy, and grumpy.

Greg hated it when the two of them teamed up. "What you want to do is called glamping," he muttered.

Stacy was not deterred. "Every camping store I've ever been in sells a solar shower and compact inflatable mattresses. Besides, I thought the reason we went camping was to enjoy God's great outdoors. I can assure you that I will *definitely* enjoy those outdoors a whole lot more now that I have a nice indoors to retreat to."

Greg was not impressed.

"Well, I think everyone's getting soft around here," he grumbled.

"Now quit fighting," Mr. Meyers said. "You're mom and I didn't intend on this RV being a point of contention. We actually bought it because *we* were growing a little tired of sleeping on the ground, and in four years all three of you will be out of the house and in college and then *we* might do a little traveling on our own. Don't worry, Greg. There's a place to store the two-man tent. We'll take it with us, and you can still enjoy sleeping on the unpredictable surface of God's creation."

Greg winced a bit at his father's dig about the ground but relented. "All right," he said. However, he still felt slighted and resentful. This would put an end to *true* camping.

"Now," said Mr. Meyers excitedly. "Who'd like to see the inside?"

"I would! I would!" Stacy and Shelly yelled in unison.

Mr. Meyers laughed. "All right then. This way please."

He opened the door and the girls climbed in.

"Man, look at all this," Stacy said excitedly. "It even has a microwave!"

Greg groaned. So much for campfire cooking.

"When can we use it?" Shelly asked.

Mr. Meyers looked at his wife who had followed them

in, and there was a twinkle in his eye.

"Well, we have a three-day weekend coming up; we thought we'd head for the coast. Stay in the Redwoods," he said.

"YES!" Stacy and Shelly shouted, and even Greg felt a twinge of excitement.

• • •

Despite the RV fiasco, Greg could hardly wait for Friday. They had been cleaning and loading the RV all week and were planning to leave as soon as school was out. Within minutes everyone was ready, and the family climbed in and headed across the mountains.

They arrived around six with just enough light to find a camp spot big enough for the RV and with a grassy spot for Greg to set up his tent. His father leveled the RV while Greg pitched his tent.

It's beautiful here, Greg thought. With its huge ferns and towering redwoods, Prairie Creek was one of his favorite places to camp. Then he turned around and saw the huge metal side of the RV and felt his stomach churn. What a blot on the scenery.

To his parents' credit, they ate outside under the stars and even though most of the meal was prepared inside, the hamburgers were cooked over the old barbecue. The campfire was lit, and the rest of the evening was spent around it, talking and roasting marshmallows. Stacy and

Shelly had never chattered so much, and Greg wished they would just be quiet so that he could enjoy nature's voice instead of theirs. Finally his father interrupted them.

"How about hiking the James Irvine trail over to Gold Bluff Beach tomorrow?" he asked.

"Yeah!" Greg said enthusiastically. That was a twelve-mile hike round trip.

"How about the rest of you?" Mr. Meyers asked.

"I'm game," said Mrs. Meyers.

"Me too," Shelly answered.

"Me three," said Stacy.

"Then let's get to bed," he suggested, and everyone, except Greg, disappeared into the RV. Greg watched the door close behind them and then sat in the semi-quiet of the night. He could hear their muted voices and saw the vehicle shake as they moved around getting ready. He shook his head.

"It's not right," he grumbled. "It's just not right. Breaking tradition. Breaking up the family." He knew that last statement was a bit of a stretch but didn't care. That's what it felt like.

He banked the fire and headed for his tent.

• • •

The hike did much to soothe Greg's hurt feelings. Physical activity had always good for getting his mind off his problems. It would have been perfect had Stacy not kept verbally spouting off about the wonderful, warm shower she could take when they returned to camp. Greg told her three times to shut up, and his father told him three times to lay off her. Camping was just not the same.

• • •

Sunday morning they took their Bibles and walked a mile up to the Big Tree where Mr. Meyers led his family through morning worship.

"I want you all to turn to 2 Timothy 2:22 and follow along with me," he instructed.

Greg had no trouble finding the verse. First and Second Timothy were two of his favorite books because they were written to a young Christian man.

"'Flee the evil desires of youth and pursue righteousness, faith, love and peace, along with those who call on the Lord out of a pure heart.'" He looked over his family. "That's one reason we like to go camping. To remove ourselves from our daily routine, pressures, and temptations," he reminded them. "To strip away those things we think we need and focus on those attributes we truly need."

Right, thought Greg cynically, *so that's why you go and buy an RV?*

"We need to give our minds a chance to rid itself of outside influences," his father continued.

Outside influences! What do you call that 27-foot monstrosity sitting back at the camp?

He chipped away at the rest of his father's message, and even though the remainder of the day was spent hiking and fishing, he couldn't let go of his father's hypocrisy.

• • •

Monday morning they had time for one more short hike, and then it was time to break camp. Greg folded his tent up and stored it in an outer compartment. His nose twitched and then he took a deeper whiff.

"Phew! Something stinks!" he complained.

His father came around and took a sniff and nodded and then went inside to check his gauges. He soon returned.

"I hadn't been paying attention. Both holding tanks are full. We need to dump them. As soon as we finish loading, we'll drive over and you can help me."

Camp was soon broken, and his mother and the girls sat at the picnic table while Greg and his father went to dump the two tanks.

"What's each for?" he asked.

"One's gray water—that's the shower, kitchen sink. The other's black water—sewage."

Greg grimaced.

"We were having such a good time, that we forgot that deep inside, the tanks were collecting all the garbage, waste, and dirty water. The gauge is there to remind you it's time to clean them out." Then he smiled. "And if you forget the gauge, your nose acts as a back up."

Greg grinned wanly as he held the hose in place while his father opened the valve and the waste water gushed through.

Man, there's a lot, he thought, and he hadn't even realized it was there. It made him think about what his father had said yesterday about escaping the pressures of society. Mentally he had been doing that, but inside, in his heart, just like these holding tanks, he had been collecting dirty water and garbage and sewer until his own attitude stunk. He realized that he needed to do a little cleaning out of his own soul, and just as his father ran some fresh water through the hose to wash it clean, he needed to put more biblical truths into himself.

When they had tent camped, someone else had had to clean out the toilets and showers. Now they were responsible. He grinned in spite of himself. Maybe this RV camping had some benefits after all.

Soul Support

Sandy looked out over the deserted track with disdain. The east wind was blowing up little puffs of dust all around, and the sun was much hotter than normal for October. She chewed on the inside of her bottom lip and contemplated skipping her run altogether. After all, Kara and Jennifer weren't running. They were off having fun. Why should she be the only one to suffer through this?

She wrestled over the idea in her mind a couple of more minutes, let out a deep breath, and made a crease in the dirt on the inside of the track.

"Oh, well," she said resignedly and started her first lap on the dusty, dirt track of the high school.

Sandy, Jennifer, and Kara had started running together two months ago when all three vowed to shed at least ten pounds apiece. Sandy had needed to drop twenty, but had signed on for just ten in case her willpower dwindled. But the three-day-a-week workouts had not been as hard as she had expected. When the three of them were together, the time seemed to go by so quickly, and it really was fun running with them.

Today, however, Kara and Jennifer, and the rest of the drama club, were helping with a mock disaster drill and weren't going to make it back in time for the workout, so Sandy had decided to go it alone. Already, it had lost some of the appeal it had when done with others.

As usual, the first hundred yards weren't too bad. Her legs were fresh and her lungs had a good supply of oxygen in them. But when she rounded the first corner, the wind smacked her full in the face and sucked what air was still in her right out. Her legs had to work twice as hard, and she had to squint to keep dirt and dust from getting into her eyes.

A small reward came at the other end of the track as she rounded the curve. The wind was now behind her and propelled her down the back stretch. She tried to make this two hundred and twenty yards last as long as she could, but before she knew it, she was bucking the wind again. By the time she finished her second lap, she was ready to quit, and she fought with her conscience.

"Two laps aren't quite two miles," she admitted, "but it's better than nothing. Plus, in this wind, I bet one lap is equal to doing two." Those arguments seemed reasonable enough to win out, and she slowed down as she neared her mark in the dirt.

"Hey, you can't quit now!" someone yelled from across the field, and she looked up to see Kara and Jennifer walking toward her. She smiled in relief.

"You got back early," she said.

"We were the first to be carted to safety, so the airmen said we didn't have to stay. We thought of you, and we were having all sorts of withdrawals from not running, so we hustled right over."

"Yea, right," Sandy quipped. "Well, I've already run two."

"Well, two extra won't hurt you," Jennifer said smiling as she stretched out.

"No way," Sandy protested.

"Whad'ya have for lunch?" Kara asked.

Sandy's face went white and then red.

"All right, I'll run two extra laps," she said.

"Why? Whad'ya eat?" Kara asked.

Sandy shifted from foot to foot.

"A chef salad."

"Aaaannnd?"

Sandy scratched the back of her head nervously.

"And peanut butter M & M's," she admitted.

"Aaaannnd?"

"And what? That's all."

"That's not too bad," Jennifer claimed.

"Well, I shouldn't have had those M & M's," Sandy confessed, "but man, those little suckers are addictive. And they looked a whole lot more appealing than a handful of carrot sticks."

The other two started laughing.

"Don't be so hard on yourself," Kara said. "We'll work it off you."

The three started off together, and this time the wind seemed to have little effect on Sandy. Working out with a couple of friends sure made a difference. Had they not come along, she would have run only two laps and then felt guilty about it. They not only kept her accountable but also encouraged her. She appreciated them and enjoyed the time they spent together.

Once they rounded the far corner, and the wind was at their back, Kara turned to Jennifer.

"So what woman are you going to introduce us to next Monday?" she asked.

"Hannah," Jennifer answered.

"I'm not too familiar with Hannah," Kara admitted.

"Me either," Sandy piped in.

"Then you're in for a treat," Jennifer informed them. "She is one of the great examples of a woman of prayer."

Kara and Sandy exchanged looks and smiled. They were already looking forward to Monday evening. The three turned the next corner and headed back into the wind. All talking ceased for the next two hundred yards, but Sandy spent the time wondering about Hannah. She was excited to study about this woman and guessed that Kara was too. She smiled to herself.

The wind fell to their backs once again, and Sandy

spoke her thoughts.

"You know, I sure enjoy Monday nights," she said. "I've learned so much."

"Me too," Jennifer said.

"Ditto," chimed in Kara.

Sandy fell silent a minute and then felt compelled to say more.

"You know when we first started this Bible study, I sure felt stupid. I didn't know what to say or do. It was weird."

The other two were silent a minute.

"I didn't either," confessed Kara. "I had always thought of myself as a strong Christian, but only in a kind of vacuum, you know, like by myself. I felt really strange sharing my feelings, thoughts, and fears with you two, even though you are my friends."

Jennifer nodded. "Yeah. But you know, now I wonder how I ever managed without our little group. I mean, yes, I was a Christian, and I would pray, and read my Bible, but until we started holding each other accountable, I would forget or find it so easy to stop.

"Same here!" exclaimed Jennifer. "And look at how many women of the Bible we have studied as well?"

"Sarah, Esther, Eve," began Sandy.

"The Queen of Sheba, Deborah, Dorcas," continued Kara.

"Who do you admire most out of those six?" Jennifer asked.

"Oh, I like Deborah" Sandy asserted. "She was a leader!"

"Well, Esther's got my vote," Kara countered. "She was willing to sacrifice her life for her people."

For the next few laps, downwind, the three discussed the merits and weaknesses of each of the women they had studied, and Sandy realized how much she had grown in her knowledge and wisdom as a Christian just because of her choice of friends.

"Say how may laps have we run, anyway?" Jennifer asked abruptly. Kara and Sandy looked at each other.

"I don't know," Kara said.

Sandy shrugged her shoulders. "Me either."

"Does anyone feel tired?" Jennifer asked.

"Not really," Kara said.

The three laughed.

"Then let's just keep going," Sandy said, and the threesome rounded the corner for yet another challenge.

Spiritual Muscles

Josh maneuvered past the weight machines toward the free weights.

"Hey, Schneider!" he yelled. "You were supposed to increase ten pounds on your squats this week!"

"Gotcha, Josh. Anything else?"

Josh checked his clipboard. "Yeah, ten more pounds on the leg press and twenty more sit-ups."

Schneider let out a groan. "I shouldn't have asked."

Josh smiled. "I would have caught up with you anyway."

"Yeah. I know," Schneider said with a laugh and moved to add the additional weight.

Josh spun his wheelchair around and worked his way back through the conglomeration of human and mechanical machines, informing various lifters of their changes in workout while recording completed circuits.

A victim of spinal bifida (a spinal condition which fails to enclose the entire spinal cord), Josh had been paralyzed in his legs since birth. Though some of the sufferers could learn to walk with assistance, Josh's case had been severe enough to restrict him to a wheelchair, and after years of futile hope, he had finally resigned himself to that life.

But he was not quitter, and he wasn't about to let it stop him from the things he loved: school, photography, and sports. He was a straight A student, had already won awards for his photography, and was determined to be a college football coach.

Though his handicap prevented him from playing most sports, he had become quite an adept wheelchair basketball and tennis player. But his love was still football, and though he couldn't play, he had studied the game religiously since fourth grade. By seventh grade, he was assisting the school coaches, and now as a junior in high school, he was an integral part of the high school coaching staff. Ironically, he was in charge of the conditioning program. Though an adult was always on hand to supervise, it was Josh who designed and ran the workouts.

The guys, thoroughly accustomed to his role, gave him no guff, for his program had been key to their championship season the year before. When other teams were plagued by injuries near the end of the season due to fatigue, Marshall High had escaped relatively unscathed.

"Hey, Carter! What are you resting for?" Josh barked. "You're supposed to be jumping rope, double time, between those two stations!"

Johnny Carter began to protest, but Josh's stern look broke into an infectious grin, and Johnny just shook his head.

"Man, that guy sees everything," he muttered to the player next to him.

"You got that right," his teammate answered.

Josh wheeled between the muscular, sweat-streaked bodies, issuing encouragement and correction. He looked about the room and smiled in satisfaction. They were working hard, and it was paying off. But it was early in the year. As the season wore on, he knew the enthusiasm would wane and then the tough part would begin.

• • •

Marshall High did well the first half of the season, losing only one game. It looked like they would be heading for the division playoffs again, so the players, riding the wave of success, were more than willing to put in extra time on the weights.

But just as Josh had predicted, as the wins continued, and the end of the season drew near, and the playoffs safely in the bag, the enthusiasm for the six-in-the-morning workouts diminished. It was a situation Josh had not yet learned how to handle, and this year was worse than last.

"Man, I'm sick of this stuff," complained one player. "We've made the playoffs. Why do we still have to work our tails off in here?"

"Yeah, my legs are sore," whined another.

"This body can't get any harder," countered a third. "Come on. Punch me." He stood up, exposed his rippling midsection, and pointed to his belly. "Come on. Right here."

Like a wave, the grumbling spread across the weight room and back again, and Josh sat tightlipped, wondering what tactic to try. No one noticed Mr. Murphy, the head coach, standing by the door until a sharp whistle blast drove them all into silence. The players stared at him with uncertainty as he slowly entered the room, walked its length, and critically eyed each player. No one moved. No one breathed. Finally, he spoke.

"Bill, what's the problem?" he asked the first complainer in a deathly quiet voice.

Bill squirmed and looked only at the ground. "Nothin', Coach," he muttered.

"Be honest with me, Bill. You're the captain of this team." Coach Murphy's voice had gained a razor-sharp edge to it.

Bill licked his lips. "Well, Coach … most of us guys feel we've gone about as far as we can go with this early morning workout stuff. Look at us. I mean, we're in good shape. Josh has done a great job, but there's not much more to do for *this* season. It's almost over."

Coach Murphy eyed him levelly and nodded slowly.

"Yes," he agreed. "You guys look like fine specimens—

physically." He paused before continuing, surveying the entire room, letting his eyes rest on each player. "But I've never heard such a bunch of whiners in my life."

Unexpectedly, he turned to Josh.

"Why don't you whine, Josh?" he asked, and the players looked at their coach in surprise. "Why don't you complain about having to get up early and come to school? About having to stay up late, after you finish your homework, to create individual programs for each of these guys? Why don't you complain about having to listen to them moan and groan about the workouts being too tough and not once thanking you for what you've done for them? Or better yet," and one could hear his momentum building, "Why don't you whine about how tough *life* is, how unfair it is that you have to be in a wheelchair while all these healthy guys flex their muscles and strut their stuff while you're a prisoner to that chair? I think you have every reason to complain. Why don't you?"

The flintiness of the coach's voice caused the players to shift uneasily. Josh licked his dry lips. He knew Coach was just using him to get to the guys, that he really didn't expect an answer, just an effect. But Josh felt put on the spot, and he wasn't about to cower now. Daily he pressed these guys to demand more of their physical muscles; well, now it was time to require something of his spiritual ones.

"I guess I'm just luckier than they are, Coach," he said quietly yet firmly.

His response caught everyone by surprise, especially Coach Murphy, but he recovered quickly.

"What do you mean?" Coach Murphy asked.

Josh took a deep breath and prayed silently.

"Well," he continued. "I already know the world's not easy or perfect or fair. So already knowing that, I just enjoy what it does have to offer me and endure the curves it throws. Maybe I'm in more of a position to appreciate what comes next."

He paused, more to catch his breath than for a reaction.

"You see, Coach, I'm looking forward to heaven and that perfect body I've been promised while most of these guys already think they've got one."

The statement was not intended to be malicious or condemning. Coach Murphy pursed his lips and nodded ever so slightly. A hush enveloped the room and no one moved, though someone coughed self-consciously. Josh sat quietly but firmly upright, his eyes never wavering from Coach Murphy's face.

"Well said, Josh," Coach Murphy said quietly. He looked around the room. "All right, let's take it in for today, but I expect everybody here at six sharp tomorrow morning, right?

All heads nodded.

"RIGHT?" he asked again.

"RIGHT!" came the response.

"Okay, hit the showers."

The guys tried to jog out of the weight room to show their hustle but each involuntarily slowed by Josh's chair just enough to give him a slight pat on the back. They were embarrassed by their shortsightedness and too hearty a slap would have been hypocritical. Their reticence was sincere.

When they had all left, Josh sat alone facing Coach Murphy. They looked at each other silently, and Coach Murphy smiled wanly.

"You'll make one heck of a coach, Josh," he said.

The Race

Melinda glanced at the running shorts fluttering around the sinewy legs of the other twenty-plus runners limbering up at the starting line. Then she glanced down at her own legs. The gold shorts clung snuggly to her mushy thighs. She wasn't fat, but she wasn't fit by any stretch of the imagination. What was she doing here?

"Runners, take you marks," came the call, and Melinda felt herself pushed toward the back of the pack as the other runners jockeyed for position and then crouched, set at the starting line. She wiggled her way back in and copied their pose.

BANG! The gun sounded, and in a whoosh, half of the pack was twenty yards out before Melinda ever left the line. She willed her leaden legs into motion and plodded along trying to build momentum. The other half pushed and shoved and jostled each other until they secured the running slot they wanted. In anger, Melinda threw a couple of elbows herself and felt better. She glanced ahead. The leaders were already heading into the trees.

By the time she reached the trees, her initial pained and gasping breathing had settled into a rhythm, and her legs were responding methodically. It gave her a moment to think.

What am I doing here? she wondered. *Whatever possessed me to try out for the cross country team?*

She used the term "try out" loosely because anyone who even suggested they were willing to run six miles a day was snatched. No cuts in this sport. Still, after sixteen years of relative leisure, Melinda struggled to remember what had motivated her to voluntarily join a daily running regime in ninety degree weather. Her mind vaguely recollected a blue bathing suit that caused her body to bulge and pucker in all the wrong places.

Enough! she told herself and forced herself to concentrate on the race. For the leaders that meant race strategy—when to speed up, when to fall back and trail, when to begin their kick. For Melinda, it meant figuring out where she was, how far she still had to go, and how much energy she still possessed. She noticed the small rise in the trail ahead of her.

Half way, she consoled herself, and pumped her arms and lifted her legs a little higher for the "uphill." As she crested the "hill," she looked ahead and saw another runner disappear from her field of view.

She tried not to let it bother her. She hadn't expected to win. She hadn't even expected to place. Before the race, all she had hoped to accomplish was to *finish*. After all, she had only been running for a month and this was her first race. She had also told herself all the platitudes: Winning isn't everything. Just give a hundred percent. Even her coach had tried to prepare her for possible humiliation.

"Don't expect too much of yourself this first time," she had advised. "Just do your best."

All that had quieted her nerves somewhat, but now, as runner after runner left more distance between them and her, doing her best and just finishing didn't have the appeal it once did.

I just don't want to be last, she thought. She saw the curve in the trail that meant a downhill was coming. *I'll gather up some speed there,* she reasoned, but when she came around the bend, there was no one to set her sights on. No one to overtake. She glanced behind her. No one. Was she indeed last? She felt her heart sink, and she felt sick to her stomach. She didn't want to be last, but there was no way she was going to catch up with those other runners.

Maybe she would have to be satisfied this time with just finishing the race and then work on increasing her speed for the next one. After all, it was a miracle that she was even out here running. At least that's what her younger brother, Mark, thought.

A miracle. She felt herself blush under the flush of her cheeks. That would make two this year. Joining cross country and the first—becoming a Christian. She had been as far away from living anything closely resembling a Christian life, but God, assisted by her friend Stacy, had other ideas, and little by little over the past year, Stacy moved closer and closer to a decision, until last spring, ready to jettison all her worries and anxieties for the peace Stacy had, she had taken that leap of faith—and hadn't regretted it. Well ... there were still tough times ... and some additional temptations ... and a few taunts ... but the peace that came with knowing God had everything under control was worth it all.

Stacy was also the reason she was running today.

"It will be good for you," she had insisted, "and we can do it together."

Melinda now thought about that. She didn't think coughing up a lung was actually good for you, and they had *never* run together. Stacy was up front ... with the leaders, while Melinda was back here ... in last place.

But cross country and the desire to be swift and svelte had proven to be a very real metaphor for her fledgling Christian walk. Just take it day by day, step by step. And sometimes, like right now in this race, all she was focused on was to keep going.

She heard something. She tilted her head slightly to cut the wind noise. Yup. She heard it again. She turned and glanced back and her eyes opened wider. She *wasn't* last. There was a runner behind her. Despite the coach's order to keep her head forward, Melinda took time to appraise her competition, and her eyes narrowed. This girl was fat. Not big boned, but fat. And she was gaining on her.

Melinda turned around and started pushing herself harder. It was one thing to come in last. It was quite another to lose to a fat girl. She wouldn't. She *couldn't*. The footsteps grew closer and Melinda felt her heart pound in her chest.

NO! she told herself and pumped harder. She felt like she was running sixty miles an hour and that her lungs would burst at any moment, and yet the other girl kept gaining on her. She could feel her labored breathing right behind her.

Melinda kicked it into overdrive and rounded the final curve. This wasn't fun, she told herself. It was one thing to jog three miles and feel like you worked off a few pounds. It was quite another to be in the race for your life, breathing tidbits of leftover air that your lungs didn't get the first time.

She glanced over her shoulder. The girl was right there. Melinda looked ahead. Where was the finish line? Her legs ached, her lungs burned, her arms felt like dead weights. She felt, then saw her nemesis come into her peripheral vision. She didn't have anything left; she knew she didn't.

The girl pulled even, right when the finish line came into view.

I can't lose, Melinda screamed inwardly, and from

somewhere deep inside she found one more ounce of energy and transformed that into a minuscule burst of power.

The way the coaches and other runners were milling around the finish line, it was obvious that the "real" race had been over for a while now. Most were oblivious to the death struggle taking place on the final stretch. Those that did turn to watch saw what appeared to be two very tired girls stumbling toward the finish line. They had no idea of the physical and mental competition taking place.

Though her eyes were blurry from the strain and sweat, and her body faint from lack of oxygen, Melinda knew she was close, and she leaned forward and lifted her plodding feet a little faster. But not until a few yards from the line did the other girl fade from view.

Melinda crossed the line and her legs gave out. She didn't fall, but she wobbled over to the nearest tree to support herself. A few seconds later, her competitor wobble up, gasping for air. Melinda looked over at her. The girl looked back and though still trying to catch her breath managed a weak smile.

"Good race," she wheezed.

Melinda smiled back and nodded. "Yeah, good race."

It had been an awful race—not pretty and physically exhausting—but she hadn't given up—neither of them had. In her first race out, she had learned something. She knew she would never be the best runner, but that was no excuse not to aim at that finish line with the same desire and determination the leaders had. God didn't expect everyone to be the star, but He did expect all to "run in such a way as to get the prize." Another metaphorical parallel she realized.

Melinda glanced over at the other girl and felt embarrassed. Less than thirty minutes ago, her only motivation was not to be beaten by a fat girl. It should have been more. Regardless of how the rest of the season's races turned out; regardless if she lost ten pounds or morphed into a model's figure; regardless of what happened in the world of cross country; in the world of Christianity, she had a lot of work to do.

The two weary runners locked eyes and Melinda realized that they would probably be seeing a lot of each other over the course of the season, and both would be fitter by the end of it. In more ways than one.

The War of the Carrots

"I won't"
"You will."
"I won't!"
"Oh, yes you will!"
"Oh, no I won't!"
"Why you little—"

Words evaded me. I was in a face-off with a three-year-old over the virtues of eating his carrots. His mother had directed that he eat all of his vegetables or no ice cream.

At the time it hadn't seemed like much of a problem. And when dinner came around, being the prudent babysitter I was, I put only five—count 'em—five of the limp orange things on his plate. But there they lay, all five of them, shriveling up and drying before our eyes while the two of us battled wills.

Cameron had tried to run wide around the table and beat me to the freezer, one of those on the bottom of the refrigerator that he could get into, but I had expected such a move. I deftly beat him to it and positioned myself right in front of the refrigerator and stared him down, but it didn't phase him. He spread his little legs, put his hands defiantly on his hips, and set his mouth in a firm, stubborn line. The line had been drawn. The battle begun.

I, for one, couldn't believe I was waging war against a three-year-old, and second, couldn't believe I didn't know how to win. There I was, sixteen years old with eleven good years of education behind me, and I was on even ground with this headstrong child.

"You're supposed to do the dishes," Cameron announced.

"You're supposed to take a bath," I shot back.

Neither of us moved, but his little lower lip twitched.

"My mom doesn't like babysitters that are mean to me."

"Your mom hasn't seen mean yet."

His eyes widened, and I felt like I had gained a foothold.

"I'm going to tell my mommy!" he said, and I saw little tears forming in his eyes.

I didn't flinch. I leaned forward, drawing close to his face.

"So will I," I hissed. He drew back.

"I hate you!" he yelled and ran from the room.

I straightened up, my victory having an unsatisfying hollowness to it. Sure Cameron hadn't won and didn't get his ice cream, but he also hadn't eaten his carrots, so what had I gained?

I raised up, relinquished my post, and began clearing

the table. Cameron was right; I was supposed to do the dishes. I looked at the five meager carrot slices on his plate. How much easier would it have been had he just agreed to eat them. Sure they probably tasted terrible to a three-year-old, but think of the sweet taste of dessert that would have followed. Surely it was worth it.

I carried the dish over to the sink and was just beginning to scrape the loathsome veggies down the disposal when a sniffling Cameron appeared in the doorway.

"I'll eat 'em" he said, but the rebellion was still very clear in his voice.

I lowered the plate, and he picked up a carrot between his fingers. He reluctantly put it in his mouth and began to chew. His face twisted in apparent agony, but he said nothing and finally swallowed hard. He reached for another, and the process began again. After four were downed, he looked up at me. Now was not the time for me to relent. It was all or nothing. There was a moment of tense waiting while we eyed each other, and then he reached for the last carrot slice and ate it. I breathed a sigh of relief.

"Thank you," I said and smiled warmly. "Now how about some ice cream?"

Cameron nodded but did not smile. He was not willing to call a truce yet. I opened the freezer door and he peered in, his little mouth puckering in thought as he looked over the selection.

"Hard to choose, isn't it?" I asked, and he nodded.

"Well, why don't you pick one for now and then before you go to bed, maybe we could share another.

He looked up at me in amazement.

"Your mom only said you couldn't have ice cream until *after* you had eaten your vegetables," I said by way of explanation. "She said nothing about how much ice cream you could have."

The wall of adversity fell, and Cameron went for a Fudgsicle. I smiled to myself. *Had I been too soft?* I wondered. I decided I hadn't. After all, such a sacrifice deserved a reward.

I watched Cameron and thought about myself. I was as stubborn and willful as he was, only not about carrots any more. Now it was about curfew and friends, cars and phones.

The television was on, a Charlie Brown Easter special, and I thought again about willfulness. How fortunate for us that Christ did not succumb to that same human failing. If He had, He might not have submitted to God's will. He might have let Peter try and slash their way out of it. He might have taken the advice of the mockers and saved Himself from the darkness and pain of the cross. He might have avoided His death completely, and then where would we be? Still offering sacrifices, still trying to prove ourselves worthy, still dying in sin.

I looked at Cameron trying to savor every drip of his

Fudgsicle, but he couldn't. There was too much there. For him, it was a major sacrifice to eat those carrots. During the time he refused and even while he was eating them, our relationship was on shaky ground.

But once he had submitted, he discovered the reward was even more than he expected, more than he could enjoy, and our relationship and his trust in me became better than ever.

As I placed his dish in the dishwasher, I prayed that I might be submissive—not as Cameron, digging in his heels until the last possible moment, but as Christ who willingly submitted to the will of His father. In that way, I would build a better, closer, stronger relationship with Him and enjoy all He had to offer.

Then Sings My Soul

I opened my hymnal to page sixteen, "How Great Thou Art," and cleared my throat. When the pianist finished the prelude, and the worship minister's hand came down, I and two hundred others lifted our voices in praise.

"Oh Lord my God, when I in awesome wonder, consider all the worlds Thy hands have made."

I glanced at my father, whose rich baritone filled the sanctuary, and smiled. He smiled back. It was from Dad that I inherited my voice—a soft, pure alto. I loved to sing, and Dad and I had performed a couple of duets together.

We started the second half of the first stanza, and I looked at Mom. Her face was beaming as she gazed up at the cross behind the pulpit. She knew the words by heart, and she glowed, her eyes shining, and her hands moving in front of her as her lips formed each word. But no sound came out. Mom was deaf and mute, since birth. I turned back to my hymnal with a twinge of familiar anguish just in time for the chorus.

"Then sings my soul …" sang the collective voice.

A sharp, nasal whining, two notes off key, pierced the air, and I cringed involuntarily. Mrs. Hobart was in rare form today. I glanced at Dad and at first thought he was oblivious to her singing, but when the chorus came around again, I saw him flinch. For once I envied Mom. Though locked in a world without music, she at least was safe from Mrs. Hobart's screeching.

The chorus came around for the third time, and I watched Mom sign the lyrics as she gazed toward the heavens. As always, I wondered what she heard in her silent world.

The song ended and so did Mrs. Hobart's wailing. We all sat down, and I opened the bulletin to the announcements. The one at the top caught my attention for the second week in a row: Mother-Daughter choir and special music. Please sign up with Mrs. Christopher before next Sunday.

A latent bitterness resurfaced both at God and my mother. Why had God given me such a good voice but robbed my mother of any, thereby robbing me of something precious the two of us could share?

For the second week in a row I took my pen and angrily ran it through the announcement then stuffed the bulletin into my Bible. I hurt and I wanted to relish in it for a few minutes.

I had no idea that, for the second week in a row, my mother, whose eyes took in much more than most mothers, had seen both the announcement and my defacement of it. Had I been even a little observant, I would have noticed her lips tighten and a wetness fill her eyes. But I wasn't. I was too busy wallowing in my own misery.

• • •

That week I was busy as usual. I had a major role in the spring musical at school and had rehearsals every day. On Friday, however, Mr. Bacon surprised us with a day off. I walked leisurely home, wondering what I would do with my extra time.

Even before I got to the door I heard the piano, and I stopped to listen. The notes were slow and painfully methodical, but I thought I recognized the song. It was "My Tribute," one of my favorites.

My curiosity was aroused, and I slipped up to the door and peeked through the small side window. Inside was Mom, her back to me, laboring over the piano I had taken lessons on for ten years. She would look at the notes and then down at her hands, playing the same notes over and over.

I opened the door and slipped inside undetected. For once, Mom's sixth sense didn't work. After the fourth rehearsal, she closed the book, positioned her hands, and then started from the beginning in an extremely elementary arrangement of the song.

The first four measures were fine, but then without her knowing, her fingers shifted one key to the left and the song was ruined. Oblivious to her mistake, she kept on playing, her head swaying to a different tune.

Tears came to my eyes. Why was she suddenly working so hard to play an instrument she couldn't hear? Somewhere in her mind's ear, the song was being played perfectly, and I suddenly realized my mother had been listening to and making music for years—from her soul.

I fought back my tears and walked over to her, placing my hand on her shoulder. She stopped immediately and whirled around, startled to see me home so early. When she saw my smile, she blushed.

"Did you like it?" she signed.

"It was beautiful," I signed back, and this time a tear did fall. Mom turned back to the piano and picked up a piece of paper—her church bulletin. She held it up and pointed to the Mother-Daughter choir announcement and then looked at me tentatively and smiled. "Now you and I can be in the program," she signed.

I felt the tears begging to run free as I was struck by a rush of guilt.

How could I have been so selfish, I thought. *She is working so hard and willing to put herself up to public humiliation for my happiness.*

I was proud of what she had accomplished in just two days, but now it was my turn.

"Next year," I said and her face fell.

"I need more practice," she signed and smiled sadly.

I shook my head vehemently. "No," I said and then

signed back. "I've caught a cold, and I can't sing. That's why I am home early."

I hated lying and prayed to God to forgive me, but to see the smile return to her face was worth it. Of course, she rushed me out to the kitchen and brewed some tea with lemon and honey, which I then had to drink. I did, like a good daughter, and then slipped off to the bedroom. I had a phone call to make.

. . .

Mother's day dawned sunny and beautiful, and I made breakfast while Dad presented Mom with a gorgeous orchid corsage. Then the three of us left for church. The Mother-Daughter choir was exceptionally good, and Mrs. Carter and her daughter, Tiffany, sang a wonderful duet.

Once their duet was over, Mr. Sturgeon, the choir director, looked my way. I stood up and walked to the front. A sea of faces, gazed at me, and I suddenly felt nervous, but when I looked at my mother, my nervousness disappeared.

"I would first of all like to ask my mother for her forgiveness," I said into the microphone, signing while I talked. "I have held a bitterness in my heart because I thought the two of us could not sing a duet together." I paused and saw pain register on my mother's face. I hastened on. "But I now know that that isn't true. I was equating singing, and in particular singing songs of praise, with being able to vocalize both the words and the music. But praise has nothing to do with the tone of the voice but the tenderness of the heart."

I could hear a slight murmur in the crowd.

"I would like to invite my mother to come up and join me in our duet," I said, reaching my hand out to my mother in invitation.

Confused and perplexed, my mother just sat there for a moment, but Dad, my accomplice, gently prodded her forward. She came up the aisle, mounted the stairs, and then stood next to me and smiled. I pointed to the sheet of music on the stand. She looked and her smile grew louder. It was another song she knew by heart.

I nodded to the pianist who gave me my note, then I in my voice and my mother with her hands began singing.

"Now thank we all our God with hearts and hands and voice."

I don't know how many times I had sung that song before and not realized the order of the words—hearts then hands then finally voice.

I have no idea if the melody I was singing matched the one Mom was signing, but I knew one thing—my heart was finally in tune.

J.E. Solinski

Other books by J.E. Solinski

Battle Ready: Vol. 1 • The Belt of Truth
Battle Ready: Vol. 2 • The Breastplate of Righteousness
Battle Ready: Vol. 3 • Feet Fitted with the Gospel of Peace
Battle Ready: Vol. 4 • Take up the Shield of Faith

Though living for Jesus is always rewarding, it is rarely easy, and for teens, the pressures are often great: peer pressure, academic demands, the desire to fit in, the need to be appreciated, the pressure to conform to the world's values. The Battle Ready series is a six volume collection of short stories based on Ephesians 6:13-17 where the Apostle Paul tells his readers to stay equipped and be ready to battle a world opposed to God.

The stories in this series focus on encouraging teens to stay true to God's calling to live a pure life and on equipping them to be ready to battle a world opposed to God while reminding them of the perfect peace Jesus promises.

....

A Matter of Control

Five very different people wrestle with the ultimate question: Who is in control?

Martha Richards is a high school teacher who prides herself on her efficiency in the classroom and her ability to solve problems. Three of Martha's students—Reba Washington, Alex Kowalski, and Travis Richards—and Martha's own son, Danny, find themselves entangled in a web of best intentions that Martha creates and then tries to control. But her intervention brings unintended consequences for everyone.

In A Matter of Control, faith is tested and illusions are shattered as each of the five comes face to face with the truth of who is really in control.

In the Father's Hands • The Sequel to *A Matter of Control*

Montgomery High School English teacher Martha Richards has watched Reba Washington, Alex Kowalski, and Danny Richards work hard to realize their dreams. But what about those who have their dreams wrested out of their hands? Four individuals must come to terms with this difficult reality.

In the Father's Hands reminds the reader that though our lives might take unexpected twists and turns, God always has his loving hands around us and our circumstances.

Available through booksellers, Ingram, Amazon.com and jesolinski.com
Ask about our fundraising opportunities.

www.ingramcontent.com/pod-product-compliance
Lightning Source LLC
LaVergne TN
LVHW041606070526
838199LV00052B/3012